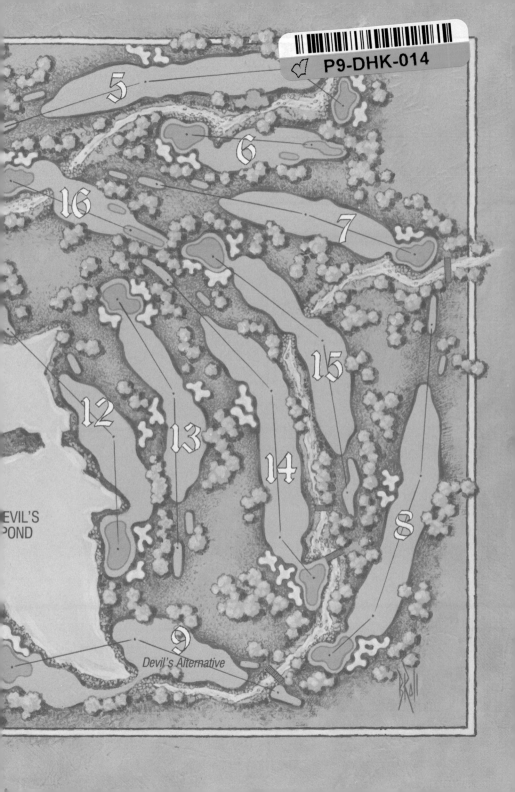

5

6

16

7

15

12

13

14

8

DEVIL'S
POND

9

Devil's Alternative

# THE
# TEN-MILLION-
# DOLLAR
# GOLF BALL

# The
# Ten-Million-
# Dollar
# Golf Ball

## Albert E. Killeen

WILLIAM MORROW AND COMPANY, INC.
*New York*

Library of Congress Cataloging in Publication Data

Killeen, Albert E.
The ten-million-dollar golf ball.

I. Title.
PS3561.I369T4   1986      813'.54      85-13760
ISBN 0-688-06096-X

Printed in the United States of America


3  4  5  6  7  8  9  10

BOOK DESIGN BY BERNARD SCHLEIFER

Dedicated to the
exasperating
intimidating
invigorating
infuriating
challenging
demanding
devastating
exhilarating
stimulating
maddening
fascinating
frustrating
wrenching
satisfying
blistering
humbling
pressing
choking
game of

# Oh, No!

**S**TREAKED WITH MUD and slush from the melting remnants of the previous week's snowfall, the station wagon traveled at a circumspect forty miles per hour along graveled Rural Route 28 toward Bainsville.

Max Sugarman drove the station wagon in a relaxed, easy manner, lolling well back in the seat, his left hand on the wheel, his right arm resting comfortably on the padded seat divider. He wore no hat. His close-cut, salt-and-pepper hair was more salt than pepper. His only concession to the outside temperature was a maroon scarf casually draped around the collar of his suit. Occasionally he would hum a few bars of "Barney Google With His Googly, Googly Eyes."

Hubert J. Carnes, the station wagon's only other occupant, shared the front seat. He kept his square frame shifted slightly away from Max and toward the window and the passing countryside. The smoke from his long black cigar fought the car's ventilation system to a standstill.

"That cigar of yours is killing me!" said Max,

and fanned the air with his right hand to dispel yet another pungent cloud drifting his way.

"You should be so lucky," replied Hubert Carnes, matter-of-factly. "These are custom-made Havanas. 'Carnesco Specials.' I buy them from a firm in Switzerland. Switzerland buys them from Cuba, and the U.S. Customs buys the declaration that they were made in Indonesia." He turned his head toward Max. "When you were a kid, did you ever collect cigar bands?"

"No chance. My mother kept me too busy practicing the violin. Have you forgotten I was to be the next Heifetz?"

"Better you became her son, the lawyer, than her son, the violinist."

Max laughed. "Learning how to fiddle never hurt me as a lawyer!"

Hubert responded with the tired smile of one who has heard that line from those same lips many, many times over many, many years. He went on to say, "When I was a kid, maybe ten or eleven, I had the biggest cigar-band collection in the neighborhood—all very neatly mounted in an album. I was really proud of it. Even then, I can remember dreaming of the day when I would be rich enough to smoke twenty-five-cent cigars." He grunted, "Now, I wonder if I was happier not smoking and collecting cigar bands than smoking custom Havanas and collecting companies!"

"And company number eleven is not far down the road," replied Max, glancing at the speedometer. "Seven more miles, in fact."

8

Hubert jabbed his cigar toward the bleak winter landscape. "What the hell is a high-tech outfit doing stuck out here in real farm country—barns, cows, silos!"

"Some very good reasons—all listed in my last report to you."

Hubert chuckled. "Max, I only read the last two sections of any report—the summary and the recommendation. If I read all the bumf in between, I'd never have the time to make an acquisition."

"As my report spelled out," continued Max, "their isolation gives them several practical advantages. First, great security. Considering the top-secret, highly confidential nature of some of their work, that's important. Secondly, isolation reduces the danger of brain drain. Silicon Valley is over twenty-five hundred miles away. There is no real competitor within five hundred miles. Then, too, they're just far enough away from Washington and the brass to discourage the casual drop-in. Besides, they have no facilities whatsoever for overnight visitors and expense-account entertainment. Most of all, their top people have farms or homes nearby. They own horses, cows, and dogs. Their kids can have fresh milk and eggs, and can go to one hell of a good private school just around the corner from the plant. Besides, Dan Finch, Bart Costain's partner, is a health nut. He loves country air and organic vegetables— yogurt, dried fruit, nuts. He even makes his own wine—elderberry. God, is it terrible!"

"I'm looking forward to meeting Dan and Bart," said Hubert.

Max laughed. "The eight-million-dollar under-statement." He leaned sideways toward Hubert. "Of all the deals I've put together for you, Hubie, this is the sweetest. Believe me—these two boys are Leonardo da Vincis, light-years out ahead."

Hubert allowed himself an inward smile of satisfaction. If Max knew just how badly he wanted to meet Dan and Bart, and how important a role they conceivably could play in his destiny, Max wouldn't be humming "Barney Google." Instead, he'd be googling in his pants.

Hubert J. Carnes, chairman of the board and chief executive officer, and controlling shareholder of The Carnesco Group—a conglomerate of ten diversified companies—managed to shut out the sound of the station wagon's motor from his consciousness, to ignore the countryside as it blurred by, to unblinkingly look ahead at graveled Rural Route 28, and to allow his thoughts to slide into the deep, overflowing worry pool that had swirled, eddied, and churned in his mind since that day some thirty-two years ago when he had acquired his first company and the beginnings of a receding hairline.

Hubert worried about the weekly, daily, some-times hourly, state of his blood pressure. He worried about the quarterly results of each of his ten companies. He worried about his increasing baldness and should he try a hair implant. He worried about another fuss with the SEC or another brush with the FTC. He worried about the competence of the security system in the Carnesco Group's new thirty-six-story headquarters building. He worried about his lack of self-discipline: eight to ten Havanas a day, always bacon and eggs for breakfast, four to six cups of coffee in the morning. He worried about a heart attack, a stroke, and cancer of the prostate, in that order. He worried about not being able to get it up, even with the occasional help of Miss Pruett, newly appointed manageress of the Carnesco executive dining room. He worried about his weight and why, at five feet eight, he could never shed those excess thirty pounds.

Yes, Hubie's mind was layered with worries, but the icing on that multilayered cake, the whipped cream and cherry of his worries, was how to rise from the vice-chairmanship and vice-captaincy to the chairmanship and captaincy of the prestigious and exclusive Quincetree Golf Club—that pampered, manicured panoply of Blue Grass and Creeping Bent—set amidst the rolling, tree-covered hills through which Quince Creek meandered with serpentine grace and devilish intent, lurking in wait for the unwary, taunting the overconfident.

Then, too, there was the maelstrom of worries revolving around the demanding layout of Quincetree and his own deteriorating golf game. Each year, less distance off the tee; too often in the woods to the right; too often in that damnable Quince Creek; that unnerving, shattering experience of shanking with his short irons; choking on critical putts; to have been a dubious seventeen handicap four years ago, and now to be an even more dubious twenty. Yet, Charles Gano Twitchell III, Quincetree's chairman and captain who was four years his senior, who never practiced, who carried only ten unmatched clubs in a disgraceful canvas bag, always managed to play to within his handicap of five.

Why? How?

At sixty-three, Hubert J. Carnes, magnate, tycoon, found the world of golf and golfing far more hazardous and uncertain than the world of finance.

His introspection was cut short by Max turning the station wagon to the right, down a tree-lined drive that led to a bisecting, high-security fence, a gate, a guardhouse, and a uniformed security guard. Max rolled down the car window to announce, "Carnes and Sugarman. They're expecting us."

"They sure are, Mr. Sugarman," said the guard, and the gate slid open. Max pulled the station wagon into one of the front parking bays designated for visitors.

Once out of the station wagon, briefcase in hand, and walking toward the entrance, Max indicated the modest, two-story building with a tilt of his head. "I told you, you were buying brains and not bricks and mortar. These guys are real bare-bone operators."

Beside the entrance to the building was an engraved, brass plaque which proclaimed:

SQUEEZE, LTD.
"WE PUT THE VERY MOST IN THE VERY LEAST."

"Not a bad slogan," commented Hubert as they passed through the double doors into a small lobby. "Let's hope they can live up to it."

A young woman receptionist, her hair gathered

12

in a straggly bun, moved quickly from behind her desk to greet them. She was very plain, very earnest, and obviously, very nervous.

"Welcome to Squeeze, Mr. Carnes, Mr. Beetman. I'm Penny."

"Sugarman," corrected Max, not unkindly. "But you're halfway right—you can get sugar from beets."

"Oh, God—I'm sorry! What a boob! It's that damn memory-training course I'm taking. You're supposed to remember names by association, so I linked your name, 'Sugarman,' with sugar beets, but out came 'beets' instead of 'sugar.' " She turned to Hubert Carnes. "How can you explain something like that?"

"I wouldn't try," said Hubert.

But Penny was determined to ride out the squall to victory. A smile and very white teeth took some of the plainness from her face. "They said I'd recognize you, Mr. Carnes, by your look of power."

"You're sure that was it, and not my cigars?" replied Hubert, holding up an unlit, ten-inch Havana.

"Oh, God! Don't tell me you smoke!" exclaimed Penny. "That will destroy them. Completely destroy them. They can't tolerate any kind of tobacco smoke, particularly cigars. This whole building is a non-smoking area. If I want to smoke, I have to sneak a drag in the ladies' john."

"They might just make an exception in my case," suggested Hubert.

"Don't count on it," said Penny. "They wouldn't let General Van Dine smoke his pipe in the conference room. God, did he blow up a storm!"

With a slight grimace of resignation, Hubert returned the cigar to his breast pocket.

Penny led them down a short corridor and opened the door to a low-ceilinged conference room, three walls of which were cork-faced and to which were pinned charts, diagrams, photographs, photographic blowups—including several of the space shuttle Columbia. The entire fourth wall was a blackboard, upon which a rough layout of a section of microcircuitry had been drawn in chalk, together with several related mathematical formulas.

Two men were seated at the near end of a long conference table that had been designed to comfortably accommodate twelve people and two computer terminals.

Both men rose at the sight of Penny. "At long last," said Dan, advancing toward Hubert with hand outstretched in greeting. He was slim, youthful, and moved with grace. His metal-rimmed glasses gave him a scholarly look. "Welcome to the land of the acquired."

They shook hands.

"Bad enough you wouldn't let us meet you at the airport," said Bart. He cocked a quizzical eye at Penny. "What happened to your buzzer? We were supposed to meet these gentlemen at the front door."

"I goofed," admitted Penny, unabashed. As she left the room, she indicated Hubert Carnes with a disapproving tilt of her head. "He smokes—cigars."

"That woman has to be a saint," said Bart. "Otherwise, why should she be on this earth to try me?"

He was a big, raw-boned, shaggy-haired, bearded

man whose bulk towered over Carnes and Sugarman and his partner, Dan. In his blue jeans, cowboy boots, embossed silver-buckled belt, blue denim shirt open at the neck, he appeared readier for the ranch or a rock concert than for the office. His right hand grasped Hubert's in an enfolding 93° Fahrenheit grip.

"A pleasure, Mr. Carnes. This is a great day for Dan and myself."

"Let's hope for all of us," replied Hubert, surprised that the brains of a Leonardo da Vinci would be housed in the giant frame of a defensive linebacker; but then he never trusted men shorter than himself.

Once seated at the conference table, and after the usual "break the ice" pleasantries, Hubert said in his best boardroom diction, "What first attracted me to Squeeze was a comment one of my executive assistants dug out for me from an article on microelectronics. It said that the unique feature of your enterprise was your ability to design both adult toys and games for the consumer market and weapons and guidance systems for the military."

Dan laughed. "Someone said—certainly not my partner, Bart—that 'genius looks at the world through the eyes of a six-year-old child.' Well, I'm the six-year-old in this company. I find toys and games fascinating. Incidentally, you'll be pleased to hear that our 'Inside West Beirut' video game is a winner. We already have a nine-week backlog of orders."

"And it all grew out of a very sophisticated training video we did for the Marines," growled Bart "But then, there is a natural empathy between high-tech toys and the Defense Department. Once you realize that most of the brass are kids at heart, then

**15**

you know why Squeeze can confound the enemy, delight the kids, and laugh all the way to the bank."

"There weren't too many laughs in your last statement of accounts," observed Max dryly.

"Nor too much cash," admitted Bart with a laugh. "Your deep pockets knocked on our door at just the right time."

Dan leaned over the table toward Hubert. "The offer you made us, and which, as Max has told you, we have accepted without qualification, is more than fair. In fact, it is damn generous. Our only concern—perhaps puzzlement would be a better word—is with clause seventeen of the agreement in which we agree to undertake a confidential feasibility study on your behalf within fifteen days of our signing the agreement."

Max, sounding somewhat aggrieved, said, "I told them you would have to explain the intent of that clause as it was incorporated in the agreement on your specific instruction, without your lawyer knowing what it was all about."

Hubert Carnes looked at Dan and Bart and gave them the confident smile that had become his business hallmark. "There are two reasons why I am happy to fund Squeeze in the belief we can take it public in a year or two. First, I am confident this company has a tremendous potential for growth and profits in the field of microelectronics and miniaturization. Secondly, your track record to date suggests that you two have the imagination and technical skills that might, and I underscore the word *might,* enable me to achieve a long-sought personal goal."

"And this personal goal is tied to the confidential study you want us to undertake?" asked Dan.

Hubert nodded gravely.

"Smart we are; clairvoyant we're not," said Bart. "Why not let it all hang out?"

Hubert smiled, unoffended. "Either of you golfers?" he asked.

Somewhat startled at Hubert's non sequitur, Dan replied, "No, that's a game I've never played. My recreational activities these days are all family-oriented—horseback riding, cross-country skiing—that sort of thing."

Hubert turned to Bart, "And you?"

"I'm for a quick sweat," was the reply. "Racquetball, handball, tennis, running. Golf never moved me. Too much status. Too little action."

"Maybe it's just as well neither of you have been bitten. Now you can evaluate my project with the wide-open eyes of that six-year-old child." Hubert settled back in his chair and reflectively looked up at the ceiling as he sorted out the words and intonations he wanted to use. "I have a dream—have had this same dream for the last three years—that one day I would find a high-tech firm, such as Squeeze, capable of designing and constructing a golf ball that could be programmed, could be controlled to alter course in flight, so that it would never be off the fairway, never in the rough, never in a hazard—a golf ball that would somehow give a short-hitter like myself that extra forty or fifty yards off the tee or off the fairway, so that I'd always be on the green, in regulation figures—a golf ball that once on the green would

**17**

go down with one putt, certainly never more than two—in short, a golf ball that would enable a duffer like myself to play in the low seventies." He looked quizzically at Dan and then at Bart. "A crazy dream?"

"Sounds wild, but not altogether crazy," replied Dan. "We've had majors, colonels, generals, sit right where you are sitting and come up with weirdies that make your golf-ball idea sound plausible and down-to-earth."

"Having been asked to design and construct a pair of exploding scissors for Castro's beard," said Bart, "a programmable golf ball doesn't appear that far-out."

Dan leaned across the table toward Hubert.

"You are serious?" he asked. "You're not putting us on?"

"Never more serious in my life," replied Hubert.

"What's the diameter of a golf ball?" asked Dan.

"One point six eight inches in diameter, with a weight not to exceed one point six two ounces avoirdupois."

"That's squeezing a big dream into a very small reality," commented Bart. He chuckled unabashedly. "But then, we are Squeeze."

"And you are talking about both propulsion and guidance," said Dan. "You want the ball to give you an extra forty to fifty yards' distance and yet you want to be able to control its flight, to be able to avoid the rough and other hazards." He shook his head. "Talented as we are, I question whether we could combine propulsion and guidance into that small a housing."

"We'll probably have to explore your idea on the basis of two separate systems altogether," said Bart. "One to propel the ball, the other to guide the ball."

"Would this project have any commercial application?" asked Dan.

"None that I know of. This project is very personal, very private, very confidential. It concerns only me—Hubert Carnes, as an individual, as a private citizen. It has nothing whatsoever to do with The Carnesco Group, nor with any of my directors, nor with any of my other business interests. All costs of this project would come out of my own pocket. My one caveat: No matter what capabilities you build into such a golf ball, to all outward appearances it must still be a regulation golf ball."

Dan smiled wryly. "Mr. Carnes, Hubert, you appreciate that at this moment in time, we are at a disadvantage. What Bart and I know about the game of golf and the technical specifications of golf balls and golf clubs is less than minimal. However, we are quick studies, and in ten days' time, maybe less, we'll get back to you and with a 'yes' or 'no.' "

"Fair enough," replied Hubert Carnes, already beginning to savor, albeit faintly, the triumphal joy a possible 'yes' might bring.

———— O ————

On the way back to the airport and Carnesco's waiting corporate jet, Max drove in scowling silence for the first ten minutes, then, without taking his eyes off the road ahead or relaxing his white-knuckle grip on the wheel, he said, "I've seen you make some bold moves. On occasion, I've seen you make some reckless moves, but this is the first time I've ever seen you make a stupid, damn-fool move."

Hubert J. Carnes smiled the malicious smile he always smiled when he knew he had embedded a nettle in Max's thick skin. "If you're referring to Squeeze, and I assume you are, I remember your telling me this morning that it was the sweetest deal you'd ever put together for me."

"What the hell are you going to do with a controllable golf ball—challenge Jack Nicklaus?"

"If those two Leonardo da Vincis—as you call them—can come up with the right answer, then I propose to use that controllable golf ball to achieve Hubie Carnes's big dream—the captaincy and chairmanship of Quincetree."

"How?"

"By winning eighteen holes of match play this coming September twenty-third, and in so doing, taking over the chairmanship and captaincy of Quincetree."

Max took his eyes off the road only long enough to look at Hubert Carnes in complete disbelief. "Are you telling me you just laid out eight million dollars to acquire Squeeze in the hope of becoming captain of some damn golf club?"

"Chairman and captain," corrected Hubert. "And the primary reason I acquired Squeeze was because of the track record those two boys are establishing. I think Squeeze has a fantastic future. The

20

other reason, and a damn emotional one for me, is the hope that somehow, some way, high technology will be able to do for me as a golfer what my reflexes and muscles refuse to do, and that is to hit a golf ball straight down the fairway for two hundred and twenty yards, and give me the chance to knock old Twitch right off his pedestal." Hubert waggled a reproving finger. "And, incidentally, Max, never refer to Quincetree as 'some damn golf club.' It happens to be one of this country's most prestigious clubs."

"And you, as chairman and chief executive officer of The Carnesco Group, one of this country's most prestigious firms, whose performance is lauded by leading security analysts as exceptional and whose shares are an institutional favorite, you're prepared to risk that kind of hard-earned reputation by rigging a golf game?"

"That game's eight months away."

"All I know is that in those snobby, goy clubs you can sleep with another member's wife and nobody cares, but if you cheat at golf or cards, they'll sling your ass out onto the street. They'll pillory you!"

"But why should I be caught? I'm assuming that whatever Dan and Bart come up with will be sophisticated; look and perform like the real thing. Otherwise, I won't touch it. And remember: This is a one-shot deal. Eighteen holes on September twenty-third, and that will be it."

"And what will you have achieved? Another chairmanship! You already are chairman of how many boards and committees and conferences?"

"Look, Max. I'm sixty-three. I've been twice

divorced. I have no children. No family. For the last nine years, apart from Carnesco, my life has been golf and Quincetree. Imagine me, Hubert Carnes, a high-school dropout, whose father was a fireman in Bridgeport, Connecticut, now vice-captain and vice-chairman of what Twitch calls the last citadel of the gentleman golfer. Four hundred acres of magnificent property. One hundred and fifty members. A club founded by a Twitchell and dominated ever since by Twitchells. I'm going to use the very same constitution and bylaws they institutionalized to keep a Twitchell always in the power seat to make it Hubie Carnes's club—a club that if managed properly could become the scene every year of the Carnesco Invitational, the richest purse in golf, with Hubie Carnes on the TV tube in his Quincetree blazer, welcoming viewers from all over the world to golf's premier event."

"I'm beginning to understand," said Max, his taut expression softening. "This time, you're after something more than just money and power."

"Status," replied Hubert. "That's what Hubie's after."

———— O ————

When Hubert J. Carnes eased his new Mercedes-Benz into the half-empty parking lot of the Carnesco Shopping Mall, he quickly noticed the dark maroon conversion van parked in conspicuous isolation from the nearest row of cars. Hubert glanced at his watch and liked what he saw: 11:20 A.M. Finch and Costain

22

were ten minutes ahead of schedule. He drove up alongside the van and after making sure that Dan and Bart were indeed the occupants, shut off the engine of his car and scrambled out, as always, wishing he could get in and out of any motor vehicle with either greater agility or greater dignity.

In turn, Bart Costain got down from the passenger's side of the van. He pushed open the van's side door for Hubert. Again, he was dressed in jeans, open-necked shirt, and cowboy boots, but today he wore a duck hunter's waterproof jacket in brown and green camouflage.

He indicated the van's upholstered interior with its couch, table, and swivel chairs. "Welcome to our covert wagon, Hubert."

Dan Finch, who had come round from the driver's side to join them, said smilingly, "Bart has yet to score with that opener, but as long as we keep using these vans, he'll keep trying."

"Who the hell buys these fancy layouts?" asked Hubert, settling himself comfortably in the middle of a couch that ran the width of the rear of the van.

"Usually, young, horny males," answered Bart, pulling the van door behind Dan and himself. "This is a love machine—a snuggle buggy—bar, couch, stereo, soundproofing, all the gadgetry necessary for conquest—but also a highly adaptable vehicle. Some people buy them to go to football games. Some people buy them just to go picnicking. Squeeze uses them for quiet business conferences in out-of-the-way places such as a military airfield or a missile site or a parking lot at the Carnesco Shopping Mall. Back at the plant, we have a van like this fully equipped for radar surveillance."

Bart and Dan swiveled their armchairs around so that they could sit facing Hubert. "Thank you for arranging to see us on short notice," said Dan, "but having reached some conclusions concerning the project you want us to undertake, we felt it important that we have a get-together as soon as possible."

Hubert said, "You've spent the last week in Florida?"

"Yes," replied Dan, "living, breathing, thinking, studying golf and only golf."

Bart held up his large left hand, palm extended toward Hubert. "These blisters attest to our devotion to the cause. Six hours of lessons from three different pros. Not even our expense account will ever know how many buckets of balls we hit, and I'm not talking about those little buckets, but the super jumbo size."

"Combine the blisters on Bart's hand with the blisters on my left heel from walking around eighteen holes with a new pair of golf shoes, and our week adds up to a painful but, we believe, illuminating experience."

"We've skimmed every book on golf we could get our hands on," said Bart. "Locke, Cotton, Player, Trevino, Nicklaus, Vardon, Snead, Hogan, Hagen— you name him, we've read him. We ran and reran all the films of the Masters plus some instructional films including the Bobby Jones classics."

"And?" posed Hubert.

"It's a game only some dour Scotch masochist

could have invented," replied Bart with unexpected vehemence. "A game of hyperbole, a game of self-flagellation, a game with a built-in ego-destruct mechanism. After one week of trying to hit that little white ball, just in the general direction of where I wanted to hit it, I am totally dedicated to your idea of a controllable golf ball, and technically, I see no reason why we can't construct one."

Dan continued, "The one publication to which we gave the most probing study was, of course, *The Rules of Golf* as approved by the U.S. Golf Association and The Royal and Ancient Golf Club of St. Andrews, Scotland, but even on first reading, it was apparent that any ball or club or playing system we might design for you would be illegal and disallowable."

Hubert nodded in matter-of-fact agreement. "No question about that, but if you remember when we last talked, my one caveat was that whatever golf ball you designed must—to all outward appearances—be indistinguishable from a regulation golf ball."

"Bart and I are already far enough into this project to know we can no longer talk simplistically about a golf ball or a golf club or a golf bag. We can only talk of a system—an integrated system—of propulsion, guidance, and control; a system that would allow you to play a round of golf over a precisely measured course in par or under, which raises this all-important question: Would you use this system, which we plan to code name 'Crossbow,' at one or at several courses?"

"At only one. My home course. Quincetree."

"Good!" said Dan, smiling in relief. "That simplifies a number of issues. Programming just one course will be complex enough."

"Where have I heard that name Quincetree?" asked Bart, his forehead crinkling in perplexity.

"It's a very old, very prestigious, very conservative club," said Hubert, somewhat pompously. "As we shun publicity of any kind, you really could only have heard of Quincetree through a member. There are only a hundred and fifty of us."

Bart snapped his fingers in elation. "I remember. Isn't that the course where Senator Twitchell died in the middle of a golf game?"

Hubert's eyebrows lifted in surprise. "You have a damn good memory. The Senator had a fatal heart attack on the sixth tee. That was eight years ago, just a year after I became a member. His son, Charles Gano Twitchell III, is our present chairman and captain."

"Yeah . . . the Senator spoke at our graduation exercise . . . hell of a good-looking man . . . tall, distinguished . . . very establishment . . . nose up in the air like he had shit on his neck."

"His son is very much the same," said Hubert dryly.

Anxious to resume his interrogation, Dan asked, "You say you would use Operation Crossbow only at Quincetree? On how many occasions?"

"Just once. Eighteen holes of match play."

"When would that round take place?"

"This coming September twenty-third."

Dan turned to Bart. "That gives us just a little over seven months to design, manufacture, and test."

Bart winked at Hubert. "That could be a squeeze, all right."

"Would this be a club tournament or a championship with a large number of players involved?" asked Dan.

"No. There would be just two of us—my opponent and myself."

"Any caddies?"

"Yes, we'd each have a caddie."

"Any marshals or spectators?"

"I doubt it. Who would want to see me get as badly beaten as I was last year or the year before? That event has become a joke at the club."

"This is the goddamnedest caper I've ever heard of," exclaimed Bart jovially. "Squeeze can't pull Crossbow together in seven months' time for less than two million, and our partner and patron saint here is prepared to amortize that amount over eighteen holes." He looked admiringly at Hubert. "You've got to be the last of the great riverboat gamblers."

"You give me a winning system on September twenty-third, and I'll consider it the best investment I've ever made," replied Hubert, storing the two-million-dollar price tag in memory for subsequent massaging of costs—but then, how much did certain politicians spend in trying to win a governorship! And what was the governorship of a state compared to the chairmanship of Quincetree!

In the dry, academic tone that came so easily to him, Dan continued, "Based on the concept work we have done so far, we are reasonably confident that we can design and build an effective system within

27

the time frame required and that all components of this system, except on closest inspection, would appear to conform to USGA regulations. Furthermore, we now know that this system would only be vulnerable to exposure or malfunction for some sixty-five to seventy-five strokes over eighteen holes of play on September twenty-third, and to only two other people, your opponent and your opponent's caddie." Dan allowed himself a thin smile. "Hubert, the odds are beginning to tilt in our favor."

Bart, planting both elbows on the table, leaned over toward Hubert. "Before we shake hands on any deal, let me throw these assumptions at you. One, that this match on September twenty-third is of critical importance to you for reasons presently unknown. Otherwise, why would you commit to possibly two million dollars and place yourself and your reputation in jeopardy? Two, that your opponent and his caddie must never know, never even suspect, how you won the game, and third, that once having won the game, you'll destroy every shred of evidence."

"I won't quarrel with those assumptions," replied Hubert.

"Then," continued Bart, "you are entering into a conspiracy of deception that involves others besides yourself. Specifically your caddie."

"My caddie?" echoed Hubert blankly.

"Yes, in our game plan, whoever is your caddie has to be a fellow conspirator. He must play a key role. Present planning calls for an infrared sensor, a power unit, electronic gear, and communication equipment to be housed in the bottom and sides of your golf bag, an additional weight over and above that of your clubs of eight to ten pounds, so your caddie will have to be strong and active. He will have to know golf and the rules of golf. He will have to be intelligent enough, alert enough, and responsive enough to be able to handle a few simple ground-station controls, but even more important, this guy will have to be totally discreet, totally incorruptible, totally committed."

Hubert looked at Bart and then at Dan. "Which of you is volunteering?" he asked.

Bart held up his hand as though commanding oncoming traffic to stop. "Don't think we haven't thought of that one, but for either of us to be that involved is out of the question."

"Who's your caddie now at Quincetree?" asked Dan.

"I have no regular caddie. The caddie master assigns you one from the caddie pool each time you play."

"But there's no reason why, no club rule why you yourself couldn't employ a regular caddie, some outsider, to caddie for you?"

"No reason at all. As a matter of fact, Dr. Middleton brings his caddie with him to the club each time he plays. So does Chauncy Fairbarns. And our chairman has his favorite caddie, old Crabbie, who's seventy-nine and can still carry a bag for thirty-six holes."

"Well, we're going to have to get out our Diogenes' lantern and start looking. We think there may be several prospects within our own company. Whomever we find, we will want you to start using

29

him at Quincetree at least two months prior to September twenty-third. We would want him to become
an established part of the scenery by then."

Bart fished out a briefcase from the side of his
chair, opened it, and took out a sheaf of sketches.
He placed them on the table in front of Hubert.

"Here are some rough sketches of the propulsion
system we would use for Crossbow." He spread the
sketches out on the table. The first sketch showed
a cross section of the head of a driver. The second
sketch showed the face of a driver, and the third sketch
showed a cross section of a tubular golf shaft and
grip.

"Each of your woods will house the same simple
power mechanism: a coil spring, made of cryllium,
one of our new wonder metals; a photoelectric cell;
plus silencer baffles and vent."

Hubert looked at each of the sketches in total
fascination. "How the hell does it all work?" he
asked.

Bart put his forefinger on the sketch showing a
cross section of a tubular golf shaft. "To load or
cock the cryllium spring, you, or preferably your caddie, will press down on this button which, as you see,
is fitted onto the top of the shaft. To all intents and
purposes, that button will appear to be the usual metal
or plastic cover that fits over the top of the grip.
As the sketch shows, a thin, lightweight metal rod
runs down the center and the length of the shaft,
and is connected at the base that is inside the club
head to this lever. By depressing the button and
inner rod downward, you exert sufficient pressure on
the lever to cock or load the spring."

"Much the same principle as a crossbow," interjected Dan. "Hence, our code name."

"But instead of a crossbow's quarrel, you will have a finely machined bolt fitted inside a cylinder just as a bullet fits inside the barrel of a gun. As you cock the spring, the bolt retracts into a position for firing. When the spring is released, the bolt is propelled forward. In fact, the bolt, when fully extended, will project slightly beyond the club face, thus exerting maximum thrust. Once the spring mechanism is loaded, the photoelectric eye releases it an instant before impact, then the bolt rams the ball, and zoom—you're up and away!

"Based on past tests we've conducted with cryllium springs, and given the length and tension of the spring we can accommodate in the head of a driver, that action alone should propel a golf ball eighty to a hundred yards."

"How far would you say you normally hit your drives?" asked Bart.

Hubert squirmed. "If I hit them straight, maybe one-seventy, one-eighty. I'm not what you'd call a long-hitter."

"Okay. Let's settle for one-seventy," said Bart. "Now, add a plus eighty yards from your spring-driven club, and you're straight down the fairway two hundred and fifty yards, right up there with Watson, Nicklaus, and Trevino."

"Christ!" exclaimed Hubert, his eyes dancing with excitement. "I've never hit a drive that far in my life."

Bart's forefinger moved to the front view drawing of the club face. "The insert we will fit into the club face showing a concentric circle bull's-eye is an accepted design and would never cause comment. However, in our clubs, the bull's-eye is, in fact, the tip of the spring-driven bolt. When the spring is cocked, the bolt retracts within the club head. The three Phillips screws that supposedly affix the bull's-eye facing in place will actually be dummies. One of them will serve as the aperture for the photoelectric eye. At this stage, we do not know whether we will need silencer baffles, but we have provided for them in case the snap of the spring should create too loud a noise."

"How many woods will be powered like this?"

"Eight," replied Bart.

"Eight?" questioned Hubert in surprise. "What about my irons?"

Dan: "There's no way we can build a propulsion mechanism into an iron, so your set of clubs will consist of eight woods, a nine iron, a pitching wedge, a sand iron, and a putter. Twelve clubs instead of the usual fourteen."

Bart: "Understand that as spring length is decreased, each wood will be graduated downward in power. For example, our eight wood may give you only ten or twelve plus yards."

Dan: "From our Florida experience, we know that if you're to get maximum performance from these woods, you're going to have to develop a swing that will assure that the club face squarely meets the ball on impact. Hitting the ball off the toe or heel of the club could result in disaster."

"How's that?" asked Hubert in alarm.

Dan: "Because the golf ball we will design for use from tee to green will not function properly unless it is hit squarely and with sufficient force for it to become well and truly airborne, and with a velocity that makes it responsive to ground control."

Bart: "The greater club-head speed you can achieve on impact, the more efficient our guidance system."

Dan: "There can be no skulling or wild hooking or slicing or shanking. You're going to have to learn to hit that ball squarely and sweetly. If you do, you can zip around Quincetree in par or under."

Bart: "That's why the propulsion component of Crossbow is our first priority. Not only do you have to become proficient in its use, but the membership at Quincetree must become accustomed to seeing you regularly play with eight woods." Then, folding his arms over his barrel chest, he intoned with great solemnity, "Always remember, Hubert, that congruity is the fabric of deception."

"We'd like to borrow the set of woods you are presently using so that your new woods will be compatible in length, grip diameter, and swing weight," said Dan.

"I only use three woods. They're in the bag store at Quincetree. We can pick them up after we've had lunch there."

"I thought Quincetree closed for the winter," said Bart.

"The course, yes, but the dining room and bar are open every Thursday, Friday, Saturday, and Sunday."

"Perfect! Bart would like to pick up your woods today so that he can take them with him to Scotland tomorrow."

"Scotland? Why there?"

"Because we've learned that supposedly one of the finest club makers in the world is one Finnie Taggart, whose shop is at the famous Muldoch links. They say if the wind is blowing, Muldoch's at least two shots harder than Troon."

"But there must be good club makers in this country," protested Hubert.

"Of course there are, but Crossbow calls for not just good, but superb club-making skills, and if our tolerances are to be observed, meticulous craftsmanship, plus the fact that Taggart has the reputation of being a very close-mouthed Scotsman and Muldoch is a long, long way from Quincetree."

"I'd simply be tying a visit to Muldoch with a business call Squeeze has to make in Edinburgh," said Bart. "If we can't make a deal with Taggart, we'll have to look elsewhere."

"Let's talk some more over lunch," said Hubert. "And we'll go out to the club in my car. I question whether this snuggle buggy would ever get past Quincetree security!"

——— o ———

Walking from the adjacent parking lot, Hubert used the back entrance to lead Dan and Bart into Quincetree's high-ceilinged locker room and down a central aisle bordered by rows of generous-size, gray metal lockers. Between each row of lockers ran a long, slatted wooden bench with a shelf underneath for shoes and an overhead rack for luggage. The carpeted floor of the locker room had, over the years, been spiked into threadbare submission.

The overall impression was one of spartan comfort but not of absolute trust, for an occasional padlock hung from locker fronts.

One sensed an atmosphere accumulated over nearly eighty years, redolent of cigarettes, cigars, and pipes, stale socks, Scotch whisky, talcum powder, foot powder, mildewed leather, sweat, caked earth, and sodden tweed, intermingled with the residue of banter, laughter, jokes, tall tales of missed putts, even taller tales of sunken putts, lamentations over the treachery of greens, bunkers, and opponents, commentary on the afflictions of advancing age, bursitis, rheumatism, sprains, blisters, stiffness, backache, and lumbago, and earthy comments on the perfidy of handicaps, human nature, and even of Mother Nature herself.

At the far end of the locker room, and adjoining it, was the entrance to the white-tiled, marble-floored ablution center—romanesque in splendor, not only in dimension but because of the large, domed skylight with the Quincetree crest outlined in stained glass, a gift in 1907 from Charles Gano Twitchell, the club's founder and patron.

Showers, basins, toilets, urinals were all in white porcelain and white marble and all in generous, old-fashioned proportions. There were enough extra-large white towels piled on tables outside the showers to rub dry the entire club membership. The bars of white soap on each wash basin were thick half-pounders, fresh-scented and unused. The array of toiletries on the white marble shelf would satisfy even the most narcissistic of members: mouth washes, shampoos, lotions, brushes, combs, powders, colognes, ointments, and astringents. However, nowhere was there the slightest evidence to suggest that a female had, would, or could violate this male sanctuary.

To the right of the entrance of the ablution center was the attendant's desk and, beyond that, the shoe locker with its receiving counter and shoe-cleaning and shoe-polishing paraphernalia.

Beyond that, the locker room opened into a small club room with fireplace, chairs, and tables, a haven for before-shower chores such as score-tabulation and correction, the payment of wagers, the quenching of thirst, and the munching of nuts and chips.

Presiding over this entire domain was Ben Spriggs, a portly, round-faced black with graying wool hair, dressed always in an immaculate white attendant's coat and always ready to flash an ingratiating smile. He greeted Hubert Carnes, vice-chairman and vice-captain of Quincetree, with deference.

"It's been too long a time since we've seen you, Mr. Carnes. Sure hope you've been keeping well?"

"Fine, thank you, Ben," replied Hubert. "I've brought two friends out for lunch—Mr. Costain here will need a tie and jacket."

Instantly, Ben cast himself in the role of a custom-tailor, and backing off a pace, critically eyed Bart's imposing frame.

"A size forty-eight should just be right for the gentleman."

He opened the closet door behind the attendant's desk to reveal a row of neatly hung, dark blue blazers.

"Brooks Brothers, no less," commented Bart.

"That's where they're from," replied Ben. "And we keep a full range of sizes. Want every guest to feel comfortable at Quincetree, particularly any guest of Mr. Carnes."

"Thank you, Ben, and come warmer weather, you'll see a lot more of me," Hubert said. "I'm going to work hard on my golf this year."

Charles Gano Twitchell, founder and patron of Quincetree, believed that large, beamed, wood-paneled rooms, each with cavernous, wood-burning fireplaces and an array of comfortable leather armchairs and sofas, gave a club the necessary air of exclusivity and masculinity. Therefore, all main rooms on the lower floor, except the dining room, were paneled—the card room in beech, the lounge in walnut, the library in oak, the bar in pine, and the billiard room in mahogany.

A stipulation in his will provided that he and his male offspring would be on view to the membership, however long Quincetree remained Quincetree. Therefore, his oil portrait hung over the fireplace in the lounge, uncomfortably cradling a wooden-shafted brassie as if it were a scepter.

Although he preferred cribbage to billiards, another large oil portrait of him hung over the fireplace in the billiard room. He also was featured in a number of black-and-white photographs of early days at Quincetree, displayed in the card room.

However, portraits of his son, Senator Charles Gano Twitchell, Jr., were even more in evidence. A large oil of the Senator, resplendent in plus fours, hung over the fireplace in the library, another over the mantel in the card room, plus many photographs of the Senator defending his constituency, his country's interests, and his own career in Washington. There were several poses of General Eisenhower and the Senator enjoying golf at Quincetree; a number of photographs of the Senator with such world greats as de Gaulle, Eden, Tito; and an especially cherished photograph of the Senator and his son, Charles Gano Twitchell III, then aged seventeen, taken at the Royal and Ancient, St. Andrews, Scotland.

Currently, there was only one oil portrait of Twitchell the Third, affectionately referred to by most members of the club as "Twitch," and this hung over the mantel of the bar. He, like his father, had chosen to have his portrait painted of him dressed in plus fours and a turtleneck sweater.

After he had shown Dan and Bart through all the public rooms and as they were about to enter the dining room, Hubert asked, "Do you now understand why some of us call it 'Twitchelldom'?"

"Impressively feudal," Dan said.

Bart chuckled. "If this is the last citadel of the gentleman golfer, you sure as hell are an endangered species."

If Hubert Carnes had been a shrine and the dining-room steward a Buddhist priest, he could not have bowed lower in greeting.

"Welcome, Mr. Carnes. I have a nice, quiet table for you."

Inasmuch as there were only three occupied tables and ten other diners in a room designed to seat eighty, the maître d's statement was redundant. However, once seated, and some distance from the others, the pervading quiet forced Hubert, and in turn, Dan and Bart, to lower their voices.

"We have a very good chef here," Hubert said, "but in order to keep him, the dining room has to stay open nearly all year round, and members are urged to eat lunch and dinner here whenever they can. Otherwise, Ferdinand might leave."

"I gather you are a very active member here," said Dan.

"I've been a member for nine years, and am now vice-captain, vice-chairman," said Hubert. The pride in his voice was not lost on either Bart or Dan. "I've worked just as hard to get almost to the top here as I have had to at Carnesco. I've been head of the greens committee, the food and beverage committee, the handicap committee, the grounds committee, the entertainment committee, not that we do that much entertaining, and—oh, yes—the finance committee."

"I suppose that's the important one," said Dan.

"Not really. This club is heavily endowed. We own all the land and buildings. That was a bequest from Charles Twitchell. The members are either rich or very rich. There's a lot of inherited wealth here. Not that that makes everyone generous, but it does make our balance sheet a very healthy one. Don't forget we sit on four hundred acres of prime real estate, perhaps the finest undeveloped parcel in the state.

Bart laughed. "No chance of a hostile take-over?"

Hubert looked quickly around the room to determine if anyone was looking their way, then said gravely, "There could be a take-over on September twenty-third. If I win that game, I'd become chairman and captain of Quincetree."

Bart looked at him incredulously. "What kind of bet can that be?" he asked. "This club must be worth millions."

Hubert hunched forward. His voice became a conspiratorial whisper. "It's a unique story. It all began with Charles Gano Twitchell, the man who put this clubhouse and four hundred acres of parkland into an irrevocable trust to be held by the Midland Federal Bank. The co-trustee is the chairman of the club, who so far has always been a Twitchell. The chairman and the bank must agree on any measure affecting the trust." A smile tugged at the corner of Hubie's mouth—"I happen to be both a director and a substantial shareholder in Midland Federal."

"What about the members?" asked Bart. "Haven't they any say?"

"Very little. We all hold certificates that entitle us to forty percent of the proceeds if the club is ever liquidated. Furthermore, the membership can elect two of the club's four directors, but the chairman, as the co-trustee, holds the right of veto."

"So your friend Twitchell is very much in command."

Hubie nodded in agreement. "Yes, for the trust agreement provides that the chairmanship and captaincy of Quincetree will be a combined office held by one man for a term of seven years. The chairman to be the co-trustee—the captain to operate the club. Furthermore, the chairman is given the right to appoint his vice-chairman and vice-captain. The one stricture: No male can become chairman until he reaches the age of thirty and no one can be appointed a vice-chairman until he reaches the age of twenty-five. Twitch's son by his second marriage is now twenty-four years of age.

"Naturally, Twitch's grandfather, Charles Gano Twitchell, was the club's first chairman and captain, but his problem was that he ate too much, drank too much, and belched too much. He was a slob and constant source of embarrassment to Charles junior, later to become the Senator. Forget the fact that daddy sent him to Yale and gave him frequent trips to Europe; nothing except his father's money meshed with Junior's social, political, and golfing ambitions. At that time, he was vice-chairman and vice-captain, as appointed by his father. Well, the old man elected himself to another seven-year term, and Charles saw that it was going to be damn difficult—maybe impossible—to ever get his father out; so in connivance with the bank, which was very much committed to Junior's political ambitions, he conceived the idea of a challenge match whereby, on September twenty-third of each year, the vice-chairman, vice-captain has the privilege of challenging the chairman and captain to eighteen holes of match play, the winner to become chairman and captain the very next day and to serve out the remainder of the seven-year term. God knows

41

how Charles junior convinced his father to accept such a challenge and to actually put it in the club's constitution and bylaws, but he did and he won, and a Twitchell has been in the driver's seat here ever since. That's why Twitch, whose son is ineligible for office for another year, selected me to become vice-chairman, vice-captain. He didn't believe as a golfer I'd ever be a threat to him on any September twenty-third, and unless Operation Crossbow is a sure winner, I never will be."

Once the white-coated steward had brought their first course and Bart had approvingly sampled his lobster bisque, he asked, "Why is it so important to you to become chairman of this club?"

Hubert belligerently thrust forward his jaw. "Because someone, somehow, has to bring this club into the twentieth century. I think I'm the one who can do it. Remember, Quincetree is famous for three things—a truly magnificent golf course, Ferdinand, our chef, and the fact that it is the most exclusive, conservative, traditional, hidebound club in the country. Twitch calls it 'the last citadel of the gentleman golfer,' but those gentlemen have to be white, Anglo-Saxon, and Protestant." Hubert laid down down his fork so that he might use his stubby fingers for emphasis. "Women are not allowed membership, nor may they play golf here. Wives and children may have dinner here, but only on Sunday night between seven and nine. This club has no professional, no pro shop. It took me three years to get a practice tee and putting green approved. This club has no swimming pool, no sauna, no masseur. The bar closes at seven-thirty every night. You need a medical certificate to own and operate a golf cart. There are only three on the premises. Thumbs down and hard on the idea of ever featuring a professional tournament here at Quincetree. That would be vulgar commercialism." Hubert paused for breath.

"But I'll bet you have a waiting list for membership as long as my arm," said Bart.

"Much longer than that. Many members here have entered their sons' applications at birth. Nobody resigns. Nobody seems to die. Last time I checked the waiting list, there was a five-year wait."

"How did you, antiestablishment as you sound, ever manage to enter these portals?" asked Dan.

Hubert grinned. "It wasn't easy. For example it took me over four years to acquire enough shares in Midland Federal to obtain a seat on their board."

———— O ————

The Monday morning of the following week, Hubert, heeding the gentle buzz of the phone on his desk, lifted the receiver to hear, "Sorry to bother you, Mr. Carnes, but there's a man on the phone who insists on speaking to you—says that it's urgent."

"What's his name?"

"He refuses to give his name. He sounds most sinister—most threatening. 'Tell Mr. Carnes this is Operation Crossbow.' "

Hubert began to laugh. "Oh, my God! I should have alerted you. Put him on." He waited for the connecting click and the bug-free green light. "Bart!

I'm sorry. Did my secretary give you a hard time? I forgot all about setting up our code name. Where are you?"

"Bainsville—at the office. Got back from Scotland last night." Bart sounded relaxed and unruffled.

"Good trip?"

"Terrific trip—both for Squeeze and for Crossbow. Managed to get over to Muldoch and meet with Finnie Taggart. What a character! Eighty-two years old and still puts in a twelve-hour day. He says it's that big bowl of oatmeal every morning that does it."

"Any interest in making our clubs?"

"Initially, total disinterest. He said he had a backlog of orders that would take him well into next year, but then we got onto the subject of Hamish."

"And what's a Hamish?"

"This Hamish happens to be his great-nephew. Aged twenty-seven. Assistant greenkeeper at Muldoch. Also works part-time at Finnie's shop. Scratch golfer—keen student of the game—supposedly an excellent teacher. Wants to come to America. Any kind of a job, preferably golf-related. I suggested that he come over to the states and act as your caddie and golfing guru from May through September. The challenge: to try and cut ten shots from your game during that period."

"Would he be my caddie on the big day?"

"Certainly he's a prime candidate. If you were to hire him, Squeeze would give him a separate contract to act as a consultant on golf-club construction. That would give us both the chance to find out

44

whether he can be trusted with Crossbow.  However, from everything I was able to gather over there, Hamish is an honest, sober, hard-working Scot who loves golf and is anxious to better himself.  Old Finnie worships the boy.  That's why he's willing to put everything aside and work flat out on our order in exchange for our giving the 'laddie,' as he calls him, a leg up."

"How does Hamish feel about such a deal?"

"He has a concern.  Until he meets you and talks to you, what assurance has he that you are, in fact, teachable?"

"What did you say to that?"

"Just what I'm saying to you—the two of you should get together and talk, and soon."

Hubert shifted uncomfortably in his chair.  He hated to be pushed, and Bart Costain was a pusher.

"Bart, this Hamish idea sounds interesting.  Give me a day or two to think it over and . . ."

Bart's voice came over the phone like a rattling discharge of ice cubes.  "Mr. Carnes—what's there to think over?  If we want Finnie Taggart to make your clubs, and on schedule, then let's use the leverage that Hamish will give us.  I can have him over here day after tomorrow.  That would be the sixteenth."

Hubert looked at his desk calendar.  Except for a manicure/hair trim at 9:00, a PAC meeting at 10:00, a United Way meeting at 2:30, and a 4:00 P.M. meeting with Max Sugarman, that day was free.  "That's a Wednesday."  But before he could add, "I'm afraid I'm . . ." Bart's voice cut in.  "What about eleven-thirty?"

Hubert bit the bullet. "Make it twelve. I'm sure to be free by then."

"Good enough. We'll be there. And, Hubert—one other piece of unfinished business—we need access to Quincetree on whatever pretext you believe appropriate so that a survey team can check the accuracy of all distances, tee to green, width of fairways, exact location of bunkers and hazards, square footage of greens. Once on the course, they could wrap up the whole job in three days."

"That's one we'll have to think through," cautioned Hubert, suddenly aware that Crossbow had come very much alive and that its machinations had already spread from Bainsville to Scotland and back to the thirty-sixth floor of Carnesco headquarters, and now threatened to move within the very boundaries of Quincetree itself. "We can't afford to raise any eyebrows."

"Congruity is the fabric of deception," replied Bart cheerfully. "See you at high noon on Wednesday."

———— o ————

Although Hubert had had no clear, preconceived picture in his mind of what a twenty-seven-year-old Scotsman from the small village of Muldoch would look like, when Bart Costain ushered Hamish Taggart into his office promptly at noon on the sixteenth, Hubert regarded him first with surprise and then with approval. Hamish did look like a Scotsman. He did look like a golfer. He was of medium height and of stocky build.  He looked younger than twenty-seven.  The thick, unruly mop of sandy hair, which he brushed back from off his forehead with a quick movement of his right hand, heightened the impression of youth.  From under thick eyebrows, a shade darker in color than his hair, his eyes were diconcertingly blue and forthright.  Hours spent in the open, braving the fierce, swirling winds that blew across the moors of Muldoch, had ruddied and freckled his complexion.  His smile was shy and constrained.

As Hubert came round from behind his desk to greet him, he thought of how out of place Hamish looked in Carnesco's executive suite.  It was not just his dress—corduroy slacks, a worn tweed jacket, leather patched at the elbows, a Vyella plaid shirt, and crepe-soled bush shoes, but rather the obvious wariness and suspicion with which Hamish, the outdoorsman, moved through the alien, thick-carpeted luxury of Hubert's office.

The strength of his grip not only surprised Hubert but made him wince.  At the same time, he was puzzled at the trace of defiance and rebellion he thought he saw reflected in Hamish's eyes.

"I'm very indebted to you for offering me this grand opportunity," said Hamish.  There was a faint burr to his speech.

"Once you've seen me hit a golf ball, you may have second thoughts," replied Hubert, indicating that Hamish and Bart should sink into the enveloping comfort of the oversize suede chairs that surrounded the large chrome and glass coffee table upon which Franchot, Carnesco's effete greenhouse keeper, had centered an enormous bowl of fresh proteas.

Hamish lowered himself gingerly to the edge of his chair and, sitting bolt upright, hands clasped on his knees, looked about in disdain at the collection of contemporary paintings and statuary that decorated Hubert J. Carnes's office.

Sinking back comfortably into his chair, Bart said, "I've explained to Hamish that we would like his help on two specific projects.  First, that you—as vice-captain of Quincetree—very badly need private coaching to improve your game so that you can better represent your club at golf."

"My game is a disaster," said Hubert, directing the confession at Hamish.

Hamish unclasped his hands and leaned forward in his chair to ask with fierce intensity, "But you do love the game?  You do enjoy the game for the game's sake—not just because you're vice-captain of some swagger club?"

Surprised at the question, Hubert replied, "To me, it's the only game.  I just wish I were a better player."

Hamish nodded in approval.

"As my great-uncle Finnie says, 'If the spirit's right, the swing's bound to come right.' "

Bart, who had been watching Hamish with the probing interest of a psychiatrist, continued in the same smooth voice as though there had been no interruption.

"Secondly, because of Mr. Carnes's keen interest in golf and through a private company he controls, he is exploring the possibility of manufacturing under

48

license a line of Finnie Taggart–designed woods. In fact, he has already involved himself in this project to the extent of ordering two sets of eight woods each from your great-uncle."

Hamish addressed himself to Hubert. "My great-uncle Finnie told me to tell you that you need have no fears about your clubs being ready on time. They will be."

"That's welcome news," replied Hubert, trying his best to somehow fashion a paternal smile that would put Hamish more at ease.

Bart concluded, "So, besides acting as Mr. Carnes's teacher and caddie, we would also want you to act as a consultant on a golf-club construction and manufacture. The two jobs would fully occupy your time."

Hamish rose agitatedly from his chair and advanced several steps toward Hubert's desk.

"You can understand, Mr. Carnes, that I couldn't give Mr. Costain here any kind of an answer until I first met you. Leaving all my kith and kin behind in Muldoch and moving over here lock, stock, and barrel is a most important decision for me. Perhaps the most important in my life."

"We understand that," said Hubert, soothingly, deftly knocking off a half inch of ash from his cigar into the marble ashtray on his desk.

Hamish waved his arm in the general direction of Bart's chair. "Mr. Costain told me about your love of golf and the out-of-doors, yet, when I look around this posh office of yours, filled with all these heathenish objects, I don't see any sign of your interest in golf or golfing or God's country-side!"

"Scenes of golf or golfing or of God's countryside don't make the front cover of *Architectural Digest,*" replied Hubert dryly, "but this office did."

"Mr. Costain talks about bringing your handicap down to single figures," continued Hamish, the burr in his speech becoming more pronounced. "But he also tells me you're sixty-three years of age. Until I saw you, how was I to know that maybe some infirmity other than your age prevented you from properly hitting a golf ball. As it is, I see you have a serious weight problem, that you're addicted to tobacco, and that you live a pudding-soft life."

"Mr. Carnes isn't planning to climb the Himalayas," interposed Bart. "He just needs to learn how to hit a golf ball a little farther and a little straighter."

"A hell of a lot farther and a hell of a lot straighter," corrected Hubert.

Hamish thrust his jaw forward determinedly. "Mr. Carnes, we Scots take our golf and our obligations very seriously. Before I can take on this job, you're going to have to tell me just how much time you're prepared to commit to working with me on your game."

"Whatever time it takes, I'm prepared to commit," said Hubert, controlling his irritation at Hamish's firebrand earnestness. He looked up in critical appraisal at the young Scot standing across the desk before him. "But you're going to have to prove that you can teach this overweight sixty-three-year-old what a golf swing is all about."

With the conviction of an evangelist, Hamish replied, "Have no fear—that I can do!"

—— o ——

Dear Hubert,

An update on our phone conversation of March 3rd—"Crossbow":

1) Cost progression as you miniaturize: Assuming an operational guidance and control system fitted in a sphere the diameter of a regulation basketball equals Y, the same system fitted in a sphere the diameter of a regulation tennis ball would cost $17 \times Y$, and the same system fitted in a sphere the diameter of a USGA-approved golf ball will cost probably $55 \times Y$. Example: Retractable fins and activating mechanism for the tee to green ball will be machined to tolerances of two hundred thousandths of an inch.

2) Delivery of your conventional bag complete with a set of eight regular Taggart woods is now scheduled for June 1st.

3) Delivery of your "smart" bag (identical in outward appearance, detail, and color to your conventional bag) is scheduled for September 1st. Your "ED" extra-distance woods will be ready at the same time.

4) Working drawings for all electronic gear to be housed in your smart bag are in process.

51

5) We have decided on an infrared system to track the flight of the tee to green ball, and we will probably opt for a "hot" ball despite the problem of having to insulate the microchip.

6) Lab tests on the electromagnetic "PS" putting-surface ball now show better than 70 percent reliability. We believe we can bring this system to total reliability within the next thirty days.

7) Bart will call you before the 15th to resolve two issues: a) helicopter mapping, and b) our fitting a battery device into all Quincetree's putting-cup containers.

8) Please note that this letter and all future correspondence will be written on chemical dissolution paper, and becomes powdered zilch seventy-two hours after receipt.

Yours,

Dan

——— o ———

The illuminated numerals of the digital clock in Hubert's study showed 11:02 P.M. Hubert sprawled comfortably in a big armchair. His slippered feet rested on the chair's ottoman. A squat, highball tumbler on the table to his right held four fingers of Scotch over ice. Within equally easy reach on the same table, a ceramic ashtray cradled a lighted Carnesco Special

The room's only illumination came from the fifty-inch TV screen placed some eight feet directly in front of Hubert, who watched the two male figures displayed on the screen in rapt concentration.

The voice emanating from the TV set's two speakers held a hint of the burr of Scotland and more than a hint of vexation.

"One more time, Mr. Carnes—stretch out those arms, elbows tight together, keep that club head close to the ground. Let your hip take you up and round. Cock those wrists. No! There's that right shoulder of yours again. Your left hand lost control."

The voice became stern. "How often are you using that rubber squeegee I gave you to strengthen your grip?"

Hubert, as the viewer/listener, winced at the contriteness of the reply. "Not as often as I should."

Righteous indignation laced Hamish's next words.

"Mr. Carnes, you're never going to get your handicap down unless you exercise and exercise and practice and practice and really work at the fundamentals of this game. That doesn't mean once a week— that means every day!"

"Shit!" exclaimed Hubert in disgust, and pushed down hard on the "stop" button of the video cassette recorder.

Getting out of the chair, Hubert shuffled across his carpeted study, switched on the lamp beside his desk, opened the thin leather briefcase atop the desk, and removed the four-finger rubber exerciser it contained. Gripping the exerciser in his left hand, he began to flex it. Turning off the lamp, he returned to the armchair. Once comfortably settled, he reached over with his right hand for the tumbler of Scotch, gulped half its contents, and after returning the glass to the table, picked up his cigar from the ashtray and began to smoke, all the while ruminatively eyeing the cassette rack atop the TV set, which held a row of video cassettes arranged in numerical sequence from Session One through Session Fourteen.

The video camera and recorder had been Bart Costain's suggestion, and Hamish had enthusiastically embraced the idea. As a result, every lesson and practice session so far conducted since the beginning of May between Hamish and Hubert on the Quincetree practice tee or on the Quincetree putting green had been recorded in detail.

With September 23 bearing down on him with the seeming speed of a brakeless locomotive, Hubert had of late been spending an hour or two each night before retiring reviewing his efforts under Hamish's tutelage to bring his handicap down to that of a ten or, at the very least, to create the illusion that his stance, swing, and follow-through belonged to that of a ten-handicap player.

The fast-forward and fast-retrieve buttons of his video cassette recorder enabled Hubert to zip through the monotonous and dreary and to focus on those moments of truth and those rare occasions where mind had triumphed over matter.

Often, he found reviewing the tapes an exercise in self-flagellation. Why did the video camera exaggerate his obesity, making his excess thirty pounds tumble out over his belt like some obscene sausage, his bumbling awkwardness, his inability to implement the simplest instruction—"Start the turn with your hip and left shoulder." His too-frequent look of total befuddlement. "What the hell did I do then?" His body's stubborn refusal to obey commands. "Head still. Keep the putter face square to the ball."

Video Tape One: After watching Hubert on camera hit some ten balls off the practice tee with an eight iron, Hamish, with grim voice, summed up the situation:

"Mr. Carnes, we have a lot of work ahead of us. To begin with, you have no left-hand connection. Your left arm collapses on every shot. Much worse, you have no turn, no pivot. Your hips are frozen. You're just lifting up the club with your hands and pushing it down with your right shoulder. No wonder you can't hit through the ball."

Hamish took the eight iron from Hubert and used the club face to rake some practice balls into position.

"Our first job is to strengthen your left-hand connection. So I want you to tuck your right arm behind your back—like this—grip the club firmly with the last three fingers of your left hand, address the ball, and then let the turn of your left shoulder and hip take the club back far enough to cock your wrist. Then, pull down with those three fingers and let your left arm and hip swing down, around, and through the ball and out after the ball." He demonstrated the shot three times for Hubert, who never failed to marvel at the fluid grace and crispness of impact with which Hamish hit the ball. "Look at my divot marks,"

55

said Hamish, pointing to the spot where he had struck the ball. "They show the club face met the ball squarely."

It took Hubert four red-faced, spasticlike jabs with his left arm and hand before he even made initial contact with a practice ball, and then it skewed off to the right in a pitiful dribble.

"Every other day, a bucket of balls left hand only," ordered Hamish, "and even more important, every day use that rubber squeegee I gave you to strengthen the grip of those last three fingers of your left hand."

"Jesus," groaned Hubert, overwhelmed at the rigors of such an assignment.

———— O ————

Video Tape Three: the scene—the practice putting green at Quincetree, late afternoon.

"For a late-in-life golfer such as yourself, the putter offers you the best chance ever of cutting strokes off your game." Hamish tossed a ball onto the putting surface and walked over to it. "Today, I want you to concentrate on putts of eight feet or under. Those are the critical putts. Those are the putts you have to make. I want you to follow this step-by-step procedure."

Hamish took up a putting stance. "First, ask yourself, 'Am I standing well over the ball?' Next, ask yourself, 'Is my stance comfortable?' Then, ask yourself—and this is very important—'Is the face of the putter square to the ball?' Then, these commands: Body still. Head still. A deliberate, firm stroke. See the putter blade face squarely meet the ball. See the putter blade move the ball forward. Do not move your head. Don't lift it even a wee fraction. And, on all putts of eight feet or under, always wait to hear the ball fall into the cup—never try and see the ball fall. Keep that head still."

Hamish then proceeded to demonstrate the putting stroke. The ball rolled into the hole. Hamish's head had not moved. He had waited to hear the ball drop into the cup.

The latter half of Video Tape Ten was one that Hubert reviewed no less than twice a week.

Hamish and Hubert were on the practice tee at Quincetree. The camera focused on full-length shots of Hubert using his new Finnie Taggart three wood.

Hamish spoke. "That was a much better shot, Mr. Carnes. You got your duff into that one for a change."

"That felt better," admitted Hubert.

"You're still not making a full turn. See if your left hip and left shoulder can't get you around . . ." Hamish's voice trailed off as Charles Gano Twitchell III walked onto the screen.

"Good afternoon, Hubert," said Charles, with his usual engaging smile. "The club is buzzing over your sudden dedication to the game. New clubs. New swing." He pointed a forefinger at Hamish. "This must be your new teacher, straight from Scotland, I understand."

"Let me introduce Hamish Taggart," replied Hubert. "He has the impossible job of trying to straighten out my game." Even after having reviewed the scene no less than a dozen times, Hubert still remembered how his face and neck had reddened as he had introduced Hamish.

Suddenly, Hamish appeared on the screen shaking hands with Charles.

"Where is your home in Scotland?" asked Twitchell.

"I come from the small village of Muldoch."

Twitchell threw back his head and laughed.

"Muldoch! I know it well. My father, the Senator, first took me there when I was only fourteen. A very testing course, and a very beautiful part of the world."

Hamish's face lit with pleasure.

"Then you must have met my great-uncle, Finnie Taggart. He's been at Muldoch these last fifty years."

"Of course I remember Finnie," replied Twitchell, and the look of approval he gave Hamish was not lost on Hubert. "The four, five, and seven iron I carry in my bag today were made by your great-uncle, a present from my father, the Senator, on my twenty-first birthday."

"I'll be damned!" exclaimed Hubert, sure every time he saw the tape that, in fact, that was the case.

Hamish reached over and took the three wood from Hubert's hand.

"Mr. Carnes's new set of woods were made by Finnie." He handed it to Charles Twitchell. "Is that not a thing of beauty?"

Charles examined the club with total admiration. "Very handsome, indeed." He turned to Hubert. "Mind if I try a shot?"

"Be my guest," said Hubert, remembering how he had nearly choked in an effort to appear affable.

With a casual dip of his hand, Twitchell picked up a ball from the bucket and tossed it down onto the grass. Nonchalantly addressing the ball, he took a slow, deliberate backswing, and then in smooth, classic style, lashed out at the ball to send it screaming out from the tee for better than two hundred yards.

He handed the club back to Hamish. "Lovely feel. Your great-uncle is a master craftsman." He looked over at Hubert's new bag with its array of woods. "Given up iron play, Hubert?"

"Let's say iron play has given up on me," replied Hubert.

Turning to Hamish, Charles said in that reminiscent tone of voice he so often used, "My father was a very fine iron player. He only carried two woods in his bag. He much preferred a one iron off the tee." His manner brightened. "And how do you find Quincetree?"

"Though I've walked it several times, I have yet to play a round," replied Hamish, "but I can tell you this—there's no course in Scotland to match it—not for layout or for condition."

Charles beamed. "You hear that, Hubert! Coming from a Taggart, that's praise indeed." He shook Hamish by the hand. "You see to it that Mr. Carnes gives you a game. If he doesn't, let me know. I'd be delighted to play a round with you."

After Charles Twitchell had left the practice tee, Hamish rhapsodized. "What a fine gentleman! And how well he strikes the ball! Did you see that slow, deliberate turn—his hip and left hand took him back and around—how he cocked his wrists at the top of his backswing. Everything I keep begging you to do, he does so naturally."

Hubert stabbed the "stop" button of the video cassette recorder. The screen went blank. Lifting his glass in mock salute, Hubert said thickly, "Screw you, Twitch!"

———— o ————

Though he sat alone in his office on the thirty-sixth floor of the Carnesco Building, Hubert's pose suggested an irrational fear of being overheard. He was hunched over the phone, the receiver tight to his ear, his other hand cupped over the mouthpiece, this despite the phone's bug-free green light showing all clear.

Bart Costain was speaking. "After he signed the nondisclosure and confidentiality agreement, Dan gave him the pitch about the Defense Department and the involvement with Crossbow."

"Did he buy it?"

"Totally. You know Dan. He can put on a convincing act, and there's a lot of 'the good ol' country boy' in Hamish. So, beginning next week, we start familiarizing Hamish with the system. When's your next workout together?"

"Tomorrow afternoon, five o'clock."

"He's sure to raise the question of coming to Bainsville next week, so give him the 'for God, country, and flag' routine."

"That I'll do. Still, no mention to him of September twenty-third?"

"No, but we'll fly that concept by him next week—the rationale, the Defense Department wants to test Crossbow against an experienced golfer such as Twitchell and over a course as isolated and demanding as Quincetree to determine whether the system can, in fact, be penetrated and whether it is malfunction-free."

"As mentioned to you before, for some reason, Hamish is a great admirer of Twitchell."

"That should work to our advantage. We'll point out to him that the Defense Department wants a foolproof, fail-proof system, and if the two of you can succeed in deceiving a very fine golfer and distinguished American such as Twitchell, then our system merits Defense's further interest and involvement."

"When am I going to get my first crack at Crossbow?"

"Week after next. You'll have to set up either an early morning or late afternoon session. We'll need to play a full eighteen. I'll walk around with you and Hamish. Dan will work tracking and control. Incidentally, we've found a place to park the van—Axminister Road, two vacant lots, nine hundred feet elevation, very little obstruction."

"That damn revolving radarscope worries me."

"God help Crossbow if it stops revolving." Bart paused. "And those hips of yours! How are they revolving?"

"I've lost two more pounds, and Hamish now rates me a fifteen handicap."

———— o ————

Hubert and Bart walked out from the rear entrance of the Quincetree locker room into the bright sunshine of a September afternoon. They crossed over the roadway toward the club parking lot, their spiked shoes clicking on the tarmac as they did so. Hamish, in slacks and open-neck, short-sleeved shirt, stood beside a midcompact car, Hubert's "smart" bag at his side.

"From here, it looks the identical twin to my other," Hubert commented.

"Hamish's shoulder will tell you it weighs nine pounds, three ounces more than your regular bag, but you're right, outwardly it is the identical twin," replied Bart.

"Good afternoon, Mr. Carnes," said Hamish, who found it congenitally impossible to address Hubert by his first name. After four months and a week in the USA, his smile was no longer as constrained. "Wait till you see all the tricks Mr. Costain and Mr. Finch have jammed into this bag. You won't believe it."

"Squeezed into the bag," admonished Bart, "and go easy on the commercials. Remember, you and I are now working for the Defense Department, and the less said about any of their projects the better."

Hamish shuffled his feet in embarrassment. "Sorry, Mr. Costain. I keep forgetting this isn't just a game of golf anymore."

Glancing around the parking lot to ascertain that they were alone, Bart reached into the top of the smart bag and ran his fingers along the inside rim. "Activating switch and communication switch are lo-

62

cated here. I'm going to switch on the power and contact control." He spoke directly into the bag. "Dan, can you read me?"

The smart bag's concealed speaker instantly reverberated with a thunderous "Loud and clear" reply, which swirled up and out from the bag's interior with leaf-shaking and window-shattering volume.

Hamish's hand darted for the switch even as Hubert, purple-faced and in apoplectic voice, commanded, "Shut that goddamn thing off!"

An eerie aftermath of quiet settled over the parking lot as the three men waited to see what consequences might result from that blast of sound, but nothing untoward stirred other than the birds and squirrels in the trees behind.

There was a rough edge to Bart's voice as he asked Hamish, "When did you last check that volume control?"

Hamish, ashen, stuttered, "Not since our tests at Bainsville."

Hubert directed his glare of outrage at both Bart and Hamish. "What the hell kind of a system are you giving me? One turn of a switch and the thing goes berserk!"

"It will never happen again," replied Bart curtly. "We'll have to eliminate the audial response and substitute a *phosphorous* screen instead. That means Hamish can talk to Dan, but Dan can only signal Hamish." Again, indicating the inside top rim of the smart bag, "We'll fit that signal panel right here and cover it with a leather flap. No problem." He turned to Hamish. "Where's your tool kit?"

63

"In the boot of the car."

"Okay. Let's do a quick fix on the volume control so that we can two-way with Dan." With an apologetic shrug to Hubert, "This will only take a minute."

Holding the smart bag with one hand, Hamish fished out car keys from his pocket with the other and gave them to Bart.

As he accepted the car keys, Bart said, "Be sure either Dan or myself gets a duplicate set of these."

Some five minutes later, volume control adjusted, the three of them started walking toward the first tee. On their way, they encountered one of Quincetree's three-wheeled trucksters. Pat Hogan, Quincetree's greenkeeper of thirty-two years, was at the wheel. Slowing the vehicle to a crawl, he shouted cheerfully, "Good afternoon, Mr. Carnes. Getting ready for the big day?"

Hubert, who considered Pat a Twitchell loyalist, and therefore untrustworthy, silently cursed Hogan for raising the issue of "the big day" in front of Hamish, but managed a pleasant "We hope to get in a quick eighteen."

"You'll find the course playing short," said Hogan. He looked up at the blue sky overhead. "We could use an inch or two of rain." Starting the truckster forward, he added, in raised voice, "Maybe we'll get some by the twenty-third."

Bart shot a quick glance at Hubert to gauge his reaction to Hogan's mention of the twenty-third, but Hubert, eyes front, lips compressed, ignored the remark and marched straight ahead.

Once they were on the first tee, Bart asked Hamish to unshoulder the smart bag and hold it in place for Hubert's inspection.

Bart began: "Hamish is thoroughly familiar with this bag and the equipment it contains. I've impressed on him that he is fully responsible not only for its operation but for the security of its contents. He is not to let this bag out of his sight or possession."

Hamish nodded gravely in assent.

Bart pointed to the eight woods and their numbered covers. "These are all 'ED' woods, but otherwise, the same as the set you've been using. As your caddy, Hamish will make the decision as to what club you will use in what situation. In each instance, he will load the ED wood as he hands it to you." Bart leveled his right forefinger at Hamish. "Give Mr. Carnes his driver."

Withdrawing the number-one wood from the bag and removing its cover, Hamish, with an unobtrusive movement of his thumb, cocked the club's mechanism. He then handed it grip forward to Hubert.

Smiling in appreciation, Hubert hefted the club. "Feels great. Same as my other Taggarts." He looked at Bart. "You're sure this baby's loaded?"

Taking the club from him, Bart put a finger over one of the three Phillips screws on the club's face. Instantly, there was a muffled, metallic click.

"Wonderful!" exclaimed Hubert, impressed.

Returning the driver to Hamish, Bart patted the back section of the bag. "Forget about sweaters or rain gear or a bottle of Jack Daniel's in this compartment. This is where all our electronic gear is housed—infrared sensor, batteries, power unit—everything that is needed for tracking, control, and communication." He shifted the bag around so that the bulky rear compartment faced the first fairway. "Hamish understands that during play, tee to green, that this rear compartment must always face the flight of the ball." He looked sternly at Hamish. "You do understand that?"

"Yes, sir."

Bart knelt down in front of the bag and motioned Hubert to do the same. With a grunt of discomfort, Hubert did so.

Unzipping the top front compartment, Bart said, "Just put your hand in here."

Hubert obeyed, only to hastily withdraw it.

"It's hot as hell in there!"

"That's an insulated, electrically heated storage chamber for the balls you will use tee to green." Bart took a ball from the chamber and held it between thumb and forefinger. "There are two reasons why we heat the ball. First, so our infrared sensor can better track it, and secondly, and even more important, as warm rubber is more resilient than cold, heat compensates for the loss of rubber wrapping in this ball as compared to the depth of wrapping you would find in a regulation golf ball."

Bart looked up at Hamish.

"The right pocket of Hamish's pants also contains an insulated, battery-heated chamber."

"What for?" asked Hubert.

"To keep this ball heated above minimal tracking temperature between holes."

66

Bart rose to his feet. "Tell Mr. Carnes the procedure we've worked out."

Hamish was quick to respond. "Once you've marked your ball on the putting green, you'll hand it to me. I'll take it from you in a towel, as though I'm going to clean it, but in that towel will be another ball—the ball I've already decided you'll use on the putting green. It will be either a regulation ball or a PS electromagnetic ball. When you're ready to putt, I'll hand you that ball and put the hot ball in the pocket of my pants to keep it at the right temperature till we're ready to play from the next tee."

Getting to his feet, Hubert addressed Bart somewhat petulantly. "You mean after what you and I went through to get our hands on those putting cups, I won't be using a PS ball on every green?"

Using his hands like an orchestra conductor seeking a pianissimo effect, Bart said soothingly, "Look at it this way. If you, as an eighteen-handicap golfer, try to fully exploit this system's potential by being on every green in regulation figures and then only taking one putt per green, by the end of the third hole your opponent will begin to ask some very pointed questions, and before the nine is over, he'll have called the sheriff. Never forget that 'congruity is the fabric of deception,' so our strategy—and Hamish understands this—is to use the system selectively, and that could mean an occasional three-putt green."

"I've got it," said Hubert. "We only sock it to him when we need to." He looked at his wristwatch. "What do you say we get this system on the road?

Otherwise, we'll never get round before dark."

"Our infrared sensor works just as well in the dark as in the daylight," said Bart, "but I agree. Let's get moving." Putting the ball he had been holding in his hand back into the insulated compartment to reheat, he took out another and held it under Hubert's nose. "You have four of these controlled-flight balls. They are all marked *HJC* in red block letters, and all have that small arrow under the letter *H.*" Taking a wooden tee from his pocket, he walked over to the blue markers of the first tee. Hubert followed him. Hamish positioned the smart bag in line with the markers.

Bart continued. "All you have to remember is to be sure that when you place a hot ball on the tee, your initials are centered and uppermost, and that the red arrow points in the direction of intended flight." He handed the ball and tee to Hubert. "Go ahead and tee it up."

Instead, Hubert turned the ball over in his hand to exclaim, "What are these?" He pointed to two thin, metal-trimmed slots on the ball's underside, spaced equidistant from what appeared to be a minuscule rivet head.

Bart replied, "Once your ball is airborne, wafer-thin fins drop through those two apertures and unfold. Computer controlled, those fins are designed to guide your ball in flight. At the same time, this sensor pin will drop into place and begin to relay data back to the computer—yardage, altitude, air speed, accuracy of flight. When your ball is three feet from the ground, flight fins and sensor pin automatically re tract."

Hubert bent down and gingerly placed the ball on the grass, aperture side up. He then looked down on it. "But you can see those slots from here! They're a dead giveaway. Anybody looking at that ball would be suspicious."

Bart walked over to Hamish and the smart bag. Reaching inside the bag, he flicked on the switch.

"Dan, do you read me?"

Dan's answer was barely audible, but there was no mistaking the unhappiness in his voice.

"What's happening? You've been shut down for the last quarter hour."

"We had a glitch on our first contact—volume nearly blew us out of the parking lot."

"Any repercussions?"

"So far, none. But I need to put Hubert's fears to rest. He has a hot ball on the grass here, gearside exposed. Can you correct? Can you get Fido to roll over?"

"Sure thing."

The ball at Hubert's feet suddenly rocked back into position, apertures underneath, hidden from view and the initials HJC uppermost, with the red arrow pointing toward the middle of the first fairway.

"I'll be damned," exclaimed Hubert in amazement and delight.

With obvious pride, Bart said, "You wanted a controllable golf ball, you have a controllable golf ball, designed to always land in an upright position, your initials uppermost. Tee it up. Send it on its maiden voyage."

With deliberate care, Hubert teed the hot ball in line with the markers.

"Let's use a two wood on this first drive," suggested Hamish, "and, before I load it, take a few practice swings." He handed the club to Hubert. "Concentrate on hip and left hand."

As Hubert began to swing the two wood, Dan's voice floated out from the smart bag. "Have you explained 'overshoot'?"

"Not yet, but we will," replied Bart. He took up a position in front of the ball Hubert had placed between the markers. "That ball and the three others you have like it are each programmed for thirty-six shots. On this hole, your drive is programmed for two hundred and twenty-five yards. But understand: For you to achieve that distance, you will have to hit the ball farther than that—say five or ten yards farther. You will always have to overshoot, so that control can bring your ball down on target."

"That's why it is so important that you stay down to the shot and see the club face hit the ball," said Hamish with great earnestness. "Otherwise, you won't get the distance the system needs."

Hubert chuckled good naturedly. "If I read you two right, I'm working for the system, not the system working for me." He handed the two wood to Hamish. "Load it up."

Taking up his stance, Hubert began a whispered chant. "Extend those arms—elbows close together—head still—let the hip take you up . . ."

With the crack of impact, the hot ball streaked straight out from the tee to split the middle of the fairway.

"Super shot!" exclaimed Bart, and then, addressing the smart bag, he asked, "How far?"

"Two twenty-six on the nose," was Dan's reply.

"What a drive!" exulted Hubert. He turned to Hamish raising the two wood aloft in triumph. "What about that hip and left hand!"

"You made a fine turn," acknowledged Hamish. "It's just a pity those extra yards aren't all your own."

Hubert's euphoria with the system and with his own golfing prowess heightened further with his second ED shot, which sped true to the green, stopping some eighteen feet from the pin. That euphoria then blossomed to ecstasy as his first-ever electromagnetic putt rattled in for a birdie three.

With the exuberance of a teenager, he exclaimed, "Wow! My first birdie of the year!"

As they walked toward the second tee, Bart said, "One of your first acts as chairman is to make sure all these putting cups are collected and dumped as far from Quincetree as possible. We wouldn't want Hogan or any of his people to inadvertently discover those battery capsules."

"Don't worry. After September twenty-third, I'm offering Pat Hogan early retirement and Hamish the job."

"Great idea. Hamish would grab such a chance."

On the second hole, Hubert was on the green for two and only some twelve feet from the hole. However, for his putt, Hamish made him use a regulation ball, marked with the same red block HJC initials as a hot ball, but without the distinguishing arrow underneath the initial *H*. He two-putted for a four.

"You were lucky to sink that last putt," commented Hamish as they walked toward the third. "You still can't resist seeing the ball into the hole. Keep that head still and hear the ball drop."

Hubert had a three on the short third.

On the long, par-five fifth, his third shot swooshed into the second of a series of bunkers that extended to the left of the fairway and outward from the green.

As Hubert took the sand iron Hamish proffered him, Bart addressed the smart bag. "Give me his position."

"Second bunker to the left of the fairway, thirty-three yards to the green and forty-one from the flag. Gear retracted, apertures clear. System now off for an unprogrammed shot."

"This is a situation we want to avoid," said Bart. "With an unprogrammed shot, you'll have no help from control. You'll be striking a hot ball with a heavy sand iron, and that might cause a subsequent malfunction. In any case, as you blast the ball out of the sand, you could drive particles into the fin aperture and render the fins inoperable."

"Why am I in this bunker, anyway?" complained Hubert. "I'm programmed to be on the green in three."

"You had a very poor shot back there," accused Hamish. "You did not make a proper turn, and your head bobbed up like a cork."

"I wouldn't take a chance on trying to hit that hot ball out of the sand," warned Bart. "They cost a fortune, and there are just four of them in the entire world. Better we save all four for the big day."

On signal from Hubert, Hamish entered the bunker, picked up the hot ball and, after wiping it off with the utmost care, placed it in the insulated pocket of his right pant leg.

As they walked toward the sixth tee, Hubert asked Bart, "Other than bunkers, what else is bad news?"

"Water, mud, sand, rocks, anything that might cause the fins or sensor pin to malfunction. If, in fact, a malfunction should occur during play, a low warning buzz would sound inside the bag to alert Hamish. I'll give you a cover-up drill on that one before we get back to the clubhouse."

"What if I were to put a ball in Quince Creek?"

"If you put a hot ball into Quince Creek, you risk not only losing a substantial investment, but if you did retrieve it and it was undamaged, the ball could have experienced a temperature drop that would make it difficult to track. Wind could be another problem—a strong head or tail wind would mean switching from computer control to manual control, and that would place high reliance on Hamish's judgment of distance and his choice of clubs."

"So, ideally, we're asking for a clear, windless day, and dry course."

"We're asking everything to work for us— weather, high-tech, Hamish, and above all, the thirteen strokes Twitchell has to give you."

———— o ————

Seven A.M.—September 23. With the first buzz of the alarm, Hubert scrambled out of his king-size bed and hurried over to the bedroom window. After a moment's futile tugging on the "close" cord, his fingers found the "open" cord, and he pulled the night blinds wide to reveal sun and a cloudless sky.

"Thank God!" he muttered, wishing that the view from his condominium apartment showed trees or flags or bunting or canopies so that he could gather some idea of the velocity of the wind if, in fact, there was any wind. He thought, "Why haven't I installed a wind meter on the roof and put the gauge right next to my outside thermometer? "Fifty-eight degrees—it'll be in the high sixties when we tee off at nine-thirty. Perfect."

He walked back across the bedroom and into the bathroom, which was large and luxurious, as befitted the chairman, chief executive officer, and majority shareholder of Carnesco. The walls were of Italian marble and the floor of nonskid Italian tile. The twin basins were sculptured in the shape of seashells, and the fixtures were in the form of mythological fish, plated in fourteen carat gold.

Shedding his monogrammed silk pajamas, Hubert mounted the bathroom scale. Still 186, but thanks to Hamish Taggart's tyranny, he had lost 14 pounds in the last forty days. He had cut down on his cigars. He now had only three cups of coffee a day in addition to those at breakfast. Stepping down from the scale, he took up a position in front of the bathroom's only floor-to-ceiling mirrored wall and addressed an imaginary golf ball. The questionable aesthetics of his tubby nakedness did not bother him. He began his soliloquy. "Keep those arms extended. Elbows close together.

"Now, let the hip and left arm take you back, up and around. Head still. Get around farther. Don't move your head. Cock those wrists. Feel that left hand. Now, down you come and through and around and out." The mirror reflected his sly smile of satisfaction. "Your swing is looking better, Hubie Carnes."

The phone rang. Hubert lifted the gold-plated receiver off its hook. It was Bart Costain.

"How are you feeling?" asked Bart.

"Fit and ready," replied Hubert, with a confidence that was part fact, part fantasy.

"I've just talked to Hamish. He says the weather is perfect. No wind at all, maybe a slight breeze from the southeast later in the morning, but nothing to worry about. There should be no dew at all by tee-off time."

"Hamish is meeting me at nine sharp. That'll give me time to take a few warm-up swings."

"Our van will be parked at the same place on Axminister Road. Dan and I will be monitoring your every shot. We'll establish contact with Hamish at nine-fifteen to the second."

"I've ordered cold lobster and champagne for the four of us right after the match."

"Who'll be the fourth—Hamish?"

"No—Twitch. After whipping his ass, I thought the least the new chairman could do was to buy him a lunch."

The marble bathroom echoed with Hubert's raucous laugh.

——— o ———

In response to Hamish's beckoning wave, Hubert interrupted his warm-up swings on Quincetree's practice tee and walked over to where Hamish was standing with Hubert's smart bag upright beside him.

"Time to test," said Hamish, and proceeded to unfasten the leather flap on the inside top rim of the bag. Letting the flap unfold, a small, rectangular panel was revealed. Hamish looked at the second hand of his watch, a gift from Carnesco, and began to intone, "Nineteen, eighteen, seventeen, sixteen . . ." Immediately after he'd reached one, a small, green circle began to flash on the panel.

"Crossbow to control. Crossbow to control. Do you read? Do you read?" asked Hamish, taking his role as an agent of the Defense Department with grave seriousness.

The word "affirmative" flashed across the panel and was then followed by "Good luck."

Hubert, peering proudly down at his golf bag and the arsenal of eight ED woods, the four red HJC balls, and three PS balls it contained, pronounced the valedictory. "You guys are tremendous—simply tremendous."

The panel flashed, "Thank you."

—— O ——

Hubert and Hamish walked onto the empty first tee at 9:25 A.M. "He'll keep me waiting till the very last second," grumbled Hubert, "just as he did last year and the year before."

"I didn't know this was an annual match you played with Mr. Twitchell," said Hamish.

"It's not really," replied Hubert, inwardly angry at his careless revelation. "It's just that Twitchell is punctual to the dot—never early, never late. As I'm always early, I have to wait."

Turning away from Hamish to face the fairway, Hubert took a deep breath of the crisp morning air and gazed out at the smooth, undulating blanket of green that stretched upward in a slight dog's leg to the right for 391 yards. The flag stick on the first green was clearly visible. The flag atop it hung limp. To his right, Quince Creek swirled and gurgled over its rock-strewn bed, offering permanent sanctuary to any ball sliced that deeply off the tee. The bank on the far side of the creek was thick with brush—maple, oak, and birch—sacrosanct from the developer's bulldozer and chain saw, as all were well within the four-hundred-acre parkland. As the fairway rose upward, the creek formed a gorge alongside so that the entrance to the first green was protected on the left by a row of formidable bunkers and on the right by the steep, downward bank of the gorge. Senator Twitchell had named Quincetree's starting hole "The Fall From Grace."

Promptly at 9:29 A.M., Charles Gano Twitchell III, dressed in houndstooth-patterned slacks, a beige cotton turtleneck, and a light alpaca sweater, appeared on the tee, followed by his caddie, who easily shouldered Charles's trademark—a scruffy old canvas bag with its ten assorted clubs and its three unalike wood covers.

The sight of Charles's caddie unnerved Hubert. Why should Pat Hogan, Quincetree's veteran greenkeeper, be carrying Twitchell's bag, and on today of all days!

As he shook hands with Charles, he asked, "Where's old Crabbie?"

"Phoned this morning he couldn't make it. Lumbago again. Pat is a last-minute volunteer." Charles turned on the famous Twitchell smile. "As the pin placement hasn't been changed since last Sunday, Pat claims no special knowledge." He turned to Hamish. "Muldoch could not boast a more glorious morning than this, could it, Hamish?"

"This would be a rare morning indeed for Muldoch," replied Hamish.

"Muldoch?" echoed Pat Hogan, blankly.

"That's Hamish's home course in Scotland," explained Charles. "A very testing layout. The Senator and I played there on several occasions!"

"You've played all over the world haven't you, Mr. Twitchell," said Pat in "I know which side my bread is buttered on" admiration.

Charles laughed the hearty, manly Twitchell laugh. "Not all over the world, Pat, but on eighteen different courses in Scotland, England, and Ireland, not to mention two courses in France, one in Belgium and over forty in this country." He took his driver from the bag, removed its shabby cover, and after handing the cover back to Pat Hogan, began to waggle the driver back and forth. "It's not the number of courses that you've played that's important. What's important is how well you've played those courses.

I'm proud to say my average score for all the rounds I played in Scotland, Ireland, and England works out to seventy-eight point nine strokes per round."

"How do you remember all that?" asked Hubert, both irritated and intimidated by the authoritative precision of Twitchell's data.

"Since I was eighteen years old, I've kept every card of every round I've ever played," replied Twitchell. "They're all filed away in my study at Stately Elms. As a matter of fact, Hubert, today will be the seventeen hundred and thirty-sixth time I've played Quincetree. My average score over those rounds, seventy-seven point four." He stooped and teed up his ball. Straightening, he said, "Well, Hubert, as I'm still captain, still low handicap, and winner of our last match, it's my honor." Then, almost as an afterthought, "I see that you've come down from a twenty to an eighteen, so my five off your eighteen gives you thirteen shots—seven on this side, six on the next." He took up his stance. "Let battle commence."

With his usual slow, deliberate full turn, immaculate timing, and powerful wrist action, Charles Gano Twitchell III boomed his first drive straight down the middle of the fairway for a good 220 yards.

"Great shot!" said Hubert, envying the autocratic authority with which Twitchell hit a golf ball. He took the driver and ball Hamish handed him and walked up to the same blue markers from which Charles had driven. The ball felt uncomfortably hot in his hand. He carefully placed it on the tee, red HJC uppermost. Stepping back from the ball, he said,

"I'm not like you, Charles. I need my practice swings."

Charles laughed. "Take your time. We have the course to ourselves."

Suddenly the fairway seemed to lengthen and narrow before Hubert's eyes. Charles's drive became a receding white dot, farther and farther out, unreachably far out. At the same time, Quince Creek seemed to widen and draw closer, and its merry gurgling changed to an ominous roar, a devouring roar. Hubert felt his guts twist and tighten. "Hip and left hand. Head still. Slow and easy. See the club face hit the ball."

Hubert carefully took up his stance, making sure the ball was square to his left heel and that his feet were parallel to the intended line of flight. He willed his head not to move, for this was the moment of truth. This shot had to be the first dividend in a stream of dividends from a ten-million-dollar investment.

———— o ————

The only conspicuous feature of the gray conversion van parked in front of a large vacant lot on Axminister Road was a very conspicuous feature indeed—a revolving radarscope on the van's roof. Drawn blinds on the van's windows hid the occupants from view.

Inside the van's rear compartment, Dan and Bart were seated side by side, knees tucked under a formica bench that ran the width of the van. Each faced their own computer, complete with screen, c.p.u., and console. Showing on Dan's computer screen was a detailed layout to exact scale of the first hole at Quincetree, "The Fall From Grace."

Bart scratched impatiently at his beard. "What the hell is taking him so long?" he asked.

Then, the crack of Hubert's driver hitting the ball came out loud from the van's stereo speakers. Simultaneously on Dan's screen, a white dot shot out from the first tee curving sharply to the right.

"It's a slice!" exclaimed Bart in anguish. "He's out over the creek."

"Then let's try and bring him back onto the fairway," said Dan, adroitly maneuvering the flight-control knob. In response, the white dot began to ease leftward in a flat arc back toward the fairway and appeared to come to rest just inside the fairway's outer perimeter.

"Nicely done," commented Bart. "How far?"

Dan punched the computer keyboard and then read out, "two hundred twenty-eight yards."

"Soft landing?"

Dan glanced at the figures that then appeared on the computer screen and read: "Gear retracted. Apertures clear. Sensor withdrawn. No adherence. Systems intact."

Bart gave two taps on his computer keyboard, and a chart giving distances to each green, keyed to all landmarks on all fairways and on all bordering rough at Quincetree, appeared on the screen.

"Hubert's next shot is programmed for one hundred and seventy yards," said Bart. "That should put him well onto the green. If he chooses to use the PS ball he'll be down in three."

"Hubie Carnes is a wild horse to ride," commented Dan with a rueful shake of his head. "On his very first shot, he pushed the system to its very limit. Next time, he may not be so lucky."

———— o ————

Walking side by side up the first fairway with Charles, Hubert found himself short of breath trying to match Twitchell's longer stride, or was his breathlessness caused by the aftershock of his near disaster on the first tee? What had he done? What had he not done to cause that vicious slice? Thank God for Dan and Bart.

Through the fog of his worry and concern, he heard Charles say, "That was a very bold, but dangerous, drive, Hubert. Until your ball began to turn, I was sure Quince Creek had claimed another victim."

"I didn't mean to cut it that fine," said Hubert, truthfully.

"And I don't remember your ever getting that distance off the tee," continued Charles. "You're hitting a much longer ball. Young Taggart evidently has helped your game."

"Oh, he's been a big help," admitted Hubert, removing the hand towel he had tucked in his belt and wiping off the sweat that had begun to ooze onto his face and forehead.

If Charles Gano Twitchell the Third was discomfited to find that Hubert had outdriven him by some five yards, he did not show it. Taking out his hand-forged Finnie Taggart four iron, which he proudly displayed to Hamish with the words,"Your great-uncle made this for me," he proceeded to hit a superb shot to the very heart of the green.

"Fine shot, sir," said Hamish. "Finnie would have liked that one."

"My father, the late Senator, ordered your great-uncle to make me a matched set of irons for my twenty-first birthday." His smile was replete with self-satisfaction. I still carry the four, five, and seven. Not many can say they've used the same clubs for forty-six years."

Hamish walked over to where Hubert stood looking intently at his ball. "Mr. Twitchell is a very fine golfer," he said. "Did you see that beautiful second of his? He used a four iron my Uncle Finnie made for him."

"I saw it," replied Hubert coldly, "but from now on, I suggest you give me your entire attention. Old Twitch can more than take care of himself."

Hamish's look of resentment flicked on and off in an instant. He handed Hubert a three wood, surreptitiously cocking the ED mechanism as he did so. "Head still, Mr. Carnes. Hip and left hand. Let the club head do the work."

This time, Hubert did manage to keep his head down, and the ball flew from the face of the club in an arching shot that swooped down onto the edge of the green and rolled forward to within seven feet of the pin.

"What a splendid shot!" exclaimed Charles, truly

startled. He turned toward Hubert and, with one hand shading his eyes from the sun, quizzically regarded his opponent as though suddenly discovering a totally unexpected dimension in Hubert J. Carnes.

Once on the green, Hubert proceeded to set the scene for subterfuge. First, by precisely marking his ball, then handing it to Hamish, who, in turn, gathered the ball into a towel and went through the motions of cleaning it. As prearranged, when Hubert was ready for his putt, Hamish would then ostensibly hand him back the same ball, although depending on the state of the game and/or Hamish's judgment, the ball could be a regulation ball, a red HJC without an arrow, or an electromagnetic ball marked *PS* in black block letters. In any event, the hot ball had to always go back into Hamish's pocket for a reheat.

As his ball was some two feet farther from the pin than Hubert's, it was Charles's putt. Once Pat Hogan had removed the flag for him and he had decided on the correct line, he wasted little time over it. Stroking the ball squarely and firmly, he knocked in his nine footer for a birdie three.

Hubert winced. "I'd forgotten what a very fine putter you are, Charles."

"Nonsense," replied Charles, modestly. "One-putt greens come few and far between for me." But it was obvious as he removed the ball from the cup that he was very pleased with himself.

Taking the ball Hamish proffered him, Hubert placed it carefully just in front of the marker only to notice as he withdrew the marker and pocketed it that Hamish had given him a regulation golf ball, an arrowless red HJC.  He gave Hamish a look of quick concern, but Hamish's expression was unreadable.

"It's a straight putt, Mr. Carnes.  Firm and to the back of the cup."

Squatting awkwardly behind his ball, Hubert attempted to verify Hamish's prognosis.  He was painfully conscious that his knees ached from his weight and that the seat of his trousers bit deep into his crotch.  Yes, it looked like a straight putt.  If only he could read greens like old Twitch.  Struggling to his feet, he began to assemble in his mind Hamish's formula for putting success:  "Are you well over the ball?  Are you comfortable?  Is the face of the putter square to the ball?  Body still?  Head still?  Firm stroke.  See the putter blade squarely meet the ball.  Listen.  Hear the ball drop."  But Hubert could not restrain his eyes from following the course of the putt and saw his ball slide two inches past the hole.

"Pity," commented Charles, relieved.  "But you have a stroke, so there's no blood."

Allowing Charles and Pat Hogan to move well ahead toward the second hole, Hubert turned to Hamish and asked in a fierce whisper, "Why didn't you give me the PS ball?"

"Mr. Carnes, that's the kind of simple, straight putt you're going to have to learn to make on your own."

"Then why didn't I?" flared Hubert.

"Because you forgot the golden rule on putts of that length—always wait to hear the ball drop— don't try and see the ball into the hole."

———— ○ ————

Inside the van, Dan said to Bart, "I think Hamish made the right decision. It's okay for a five handicap to make a birdie on the first hole, but way out of character for an eighteen."

Bart nodded in agreement. "Hubert still has to learn that congruity is the fabric of deception."

———— ○ ————

However, after the second hole was halved, Hubert, Hamish, and high technology began to trample on Quincetree and Charles Gano Twitchell III, almost at will.

On the short 153-yard third, an ED seven wood put Hubert four feet from the flag, and using an arrowless red HJC ball, he sank a tricky curving putt on his own to go one up.

At the long 525-yard fifth, three ED woods put Hubert on the fringe of the green, to face an awesome putt of just over forty feet. However, the PS ball sped across the green with deadly accuracy to hit the back of the hole and plop in for a birdie four.

"A fantastic four," acknowledged Charles, and for the first time, his pleasantry appeared to wear thin. "That puts you two up."

After sinking his own putt for a five, Charles pulled out Hubert's card from his back pocket and entered the scores. Hubert did the same.

Charles's tone held a slight reprimand. "I make you even par for the first five holes. Not bad for an eighteen handicap."

Hubert grinned impudently. "I make you one under for the first five holes. Not bad for a five handicap."

Hubert and Hamish took great care to use Hubert's shot on the sixth to simply halve the hole.

On the seventh hole, Charles Gano Twitchell III faltered in stride. For the first time in Hubert's memory, not that he had played that often with Charles—perhaps five or six times over a period of four years—Charles Twitchell hooked his tee shot into the rough and trees.

"That ball could be lost," Charles said, shaking his iron-gray mane in self-condemnation.

"I hope not," said Hubert, surprised at the depth of his own hypocrisy.

"The pressure's beginning to tell," said Twitchell, with a supercilious laugh that suggested that nothing could be further from the truth. He strode off in the direction of the ball with Hogan at his heels.

Behind Twitchell's retreating back, Hubert made no effort to conceal his exultation. "He's in the shit! Even if he finds his ball, it will take him at least two shots to reach the green." He rubbed his hands together in glee. "Here's where Hubie goes three up."

In hesitant, puzzled manner, Hamish asked, "Does it matter to the Defense Department whether Mr. Twitchell or you win as long as he doesn't suspect that we've cheated?"

Hubert's rocket of protest at the use of the word "cheated" fizzled in his throat. He said lamely, "Not really, but I know they'll be far more impressed if the system wins and wins big."

Hubert easily won the seventh, for Charles did

**87**

not find his ball and only managed to reach the seventh green in four, whereupon he took two putts for a six.  Although his ED woods had put him a scant fifteen feet from the pin for two, Hubert deliberately three-putted for the winning five.

He was still three up when they reached the ninth—Senator Twitchell's favorite hole and which the Senator had named "The Devil's Alternative," so called because Quince Creek—thanks to a dam on the left—formed a menacing expanse of water designed to frontally protect the green from all, save the bold, the foolhardy, and the competent. Therefore, any player who failed to achieve a satisfactory drive either had to play short with his second or risk putting his ball in the water, and the water of Devil's Pond was deep and the water of Devil's Pond was cold.

"In all the time I played with my father, not once did he ever put a ball in Devil's Pond," eulogized Charles.

"What a fine golfer and gentleman he was," dutifully chanted Hogan.

As he walked over to tee up his ball, Hubert exuded a swaggering confidence.  The heat of the ball in his hand reassured him.  His three-hole lead fortified him.  The knowledge that he received a stroke on this, the ninth hole, sustained him.

"Well, I've put more than my share in the Devil's Pond," he confessed.  "But not today—not the way I'm hitting them."  But Hubert, in his eagerness to excel, to demonstrate the omnipotence of the system at his command, failed to pivot, failed to stay down to the ball, failed to see the club face strike the ball, and the result was a skulled drive that flew a scant six inches above the fairway grass to then crash and crazily bounce and careen to a convulsive stop.

With thumping heart, Hubert walked over to hand the offending club to Hamish, but the sudden palor that washed over Hamish's face plus the faint, insistent buzzing sound that emanated from the bag's interior confirmed Hubert's dread fear, and a lump compounded of anguish and panic formed in his throat. Catastrophe had indeed struck—Crossbow was in the throes of malfunction.

Bart's training in emergency procedures stood Hubert in good stead.

"Goddamn that wasp!" he exclaimed, waving his arms wildly as though to protect himself from vicious onslaught, but in reality creating the required diversion to allow Hamish to slip his hand inside the bag and shut off the system. "Damn near bit me!" added Hubert, seeking Charles's and Pat's sympathy at his near escape.

"Strange," commented Charles. "We seldom have wasps this time of year."

"Might have been a bee," said Pat.

In contrast to Hubert's disastrous shot, Charles hit a long, soaring drive that came to a stop within easy range of the ninth green.

"Just like your father before you," said Pat in benediction.

The lump in Hubert's throat impeded speech, but he managed to say, "We'll move on," and proceeded to do just that, driven by the imperative that he must somehow gain the chance to inspect that stricken ball.

"Oh, my God!" he gasped in horror as he walked up to his ball, for not only was the underside of the ball fully exposed, but the flight fins were still extended and vibrating in agony. The sensor pin was bent at a sickening angle.

Hubert turned swiftly round to determine the whereabouts of Charles and Pat. They were fast approaching.

"What the hell do we do?" he asked in desperation.

Hamish jerked the cover off the bag's eight wood and in one swift, smooth movement cocked the ED mechanism and handed the club to Hubert.

"Quick! Knock it in the water."

Never in his wildest fantasies could Hubert ever have envisioned he would deliberately send some two hundred thousand dollars into wobbly erratic flight to finally splash into Devil's Pond, but he did, and he did so with profound relief. Crossbow's ruptured secret now lay peacefully at the bottom of Devil's Pond.

"That ball acted rather strangely, as though you had cut the cover," observed Charles.

"Maybe so," replied Hubert. "I hurried that shot. Just too damn anxious to get over the water and onto the green."

He took the regulation ball that Hamish handed him. "I'll drop this side and play four."

Charles and Pat walked up ahead to where Charles's ball lay, a pristine white sphere on the green fairway.

"That was quick thinking on your part, Hamish," said Hubert. "I'm proud of you."

There was torment in Hamish's expression. "I'm not that proud of myself. If my great-uncle Finnie were to see to what disgraceful use I'm putting the clubs he worked so hard to make, he'd disown me— and so would the rest of my family back at Muldoch."

Hubert put his hand on Hamish's shoulder in a gesture of understanding and reassurance.

"Forget that we're playing a golf game this morning. We're not. We're conducting a test. So far, Twitchell and Hogan suspect nothing. Let's make sure it stays that way."

Charles's second shot landed just past the flag on the ninth, but the ball failed to hold and rolled onward toward the far edge of the green.

Two club lengths from the pond's edge, Hubert dropped an arrowless HJC over his right shoulder to the ground.

Trying to calibrate the distance between his ball and the green, he asked, "What do you think?"

"It's a full nine iron," said Hamish, handing him the club. "Don't baby it."

Hubert stayed down on the shot. The ball flew high in the air to drop dead ten feet from the pin. Hubert gave a grunt of satisfaction. "I lie four, net three." He started to walk parallel to the pond's edge toward the bridge that led across to the ninth green. "With our electromagnetic ball, I can halve this hole."

Charles, in a deliberate effort to make sure his first putt was not short, overestimated the touch required and saw his ball roll well past the hole to give him a difficult uphill return. This he missed by no

91

more than the width of a blade of grass.

If his missed second putt had driven a stake into his heart, Charles did not show it. As he tapped his third putt into the hole, his aplomb was apparently unshaken, but as Hubert's ball sped unerringly across the ten-foot interval to scuttle into the hole for a five, net four and a win, Charles Gano Twitchell III rocked back on his heels and visibly aged.

———— O ————

It was a disconsolate Charles Gano Twitchell III who walked onto Quincetree's large open verandah and slumped into a webbed, aluminum chair, jarring the round-topped table beside it in the process. Hubert sat down across from him.

"You know," confessed Charles wearily, "I have never walked into this club before being four down after nine holes." He pulled the scorecard from his pocket and laid it on the table. "It's not that I've played that badly." His forefinger moved down the card. "Three over." He looked across at Hubert in reluctant admiration. "It's you, Hubert. You're playing magnificently."

Hubert shrugged off the compliment. "I've been lucky."

"Luck hasn't entered into it," said Charles, in flat contradiction. "Your long game has improved out of all recognition." He picked up the card and again studied it. "In spite of your three-putting the seventh, you still finished with a gross forty." He smiled wistfully. "I should have listened more carefully to Pat Hogan. He warned me that you and young Hamish were plotting my demise." He beckoned the white-coated steward who had just emerged onto the verandah from the club's interior.

"My check," said Hubert, disturbed at Charles's use of the word "plotting." "What will you have?"

Charles looked up at the white-coated steward. "Give me my usual pot of orange pekoe, Peter. And are the scones fresh?"

"Straight out of the oven, sir."

"All right—let me have scones, strawberry jam, and a dollop of whipped cream."

"Coffee and scones for me," said Hubert, "but make it two dollops of whipped cream."

"You've lost weight," said Charles, appraising Hubert from across the table. "I noticed it on the first tee. It has helped your swing."

"Fourteen pounds," replied Hubert. "Young Taggart has kept after me to knock off the weight."

"All part of a master plan, I suppose," said Charles, a hint of bitterness seeping into his voice. Then, leaning across the table toward Hubert, his expression changed to one of openness and candor. "I must admit, when I think back on how wretchedly you played last year and the year before, it never entered my mind that you would ever pose a serious threat. Now, here I sit on the verandah of the clubhouse my grandfather built and donated to Quincetree, and I am four down after the first nine holes." His voice cracked. "It's unbelievable!"

——— O ———

Hamish's voice suddenly filled the van's interior. "Crossbow to Control. Do you read?"

Instantly, Dan pressed the signal button in acknowledgment.

"They're just finishing tea. As Mr. Carnes is four up at the turn, we'll be using a regulation ball on the tenth, so you won't receive us till the eleventh. Over."

As Bart's fingers tapped out the letters of his reply, the message formed on the computer screen.

"Will clear first two shots from tenth program. Stop. Reestablish contact eleventh tee."

"Will do. Over and out."

"With the system working as well as it is, Hubert can afford to give back a hole or two," said Dan.

"I'm sure Hamish forced that decision," replied Bart. "A mere win isn't going to satisfy Hubert. He wants a triumph."

———— o ————

Even during his first warm-up swing on the tenth tee, Hubert found it hard to concentrate on such fundamentals as "extend those arms, elbows close together, feel the last three fingers of the left hand." Instead, he was overly conscious of those three whipped cream–laden scones—and why had Hamish and Pat Hogan kept Charles and him waiting at the tenth tee to finally appear, not walking, but idly strolling, side by side, in deepest conversation like two villagers immersed in gossip. In fact, so absorbed were they that they both looked up in startled surprise to find they had reached the tee. Yet, the imminence of victory helped remove his dark concern over Hamish's and Pat's belated arrival. The enormity of the prize almost within his reach made it difficult for him to shut out visions of the crowds that would line the fairways and greens when he established the Carnesco Open, which would be the richest purse in golf. Then, what about Carnesco Gardens, that exclusive condominium complex he would build the other side of "The Fall From Grace?" His thoughts then turned to Bart and Dan, his two loyal allies sitting cooped in their van atop Axminister Road waiting for him to drive. Max had been so right. They were indeed Leonardo da Vincis, light-years out ahead. The proof of that was that he, Hubert J. Carnes, stood on the tenth tee, four up after the first nine, and that in spite of this opponent having shot a gross thirty-nine.

The ball Hamish handed him was so hot in his hand that he nearly dropped it, but he managed to place it on the tee, red HJC uppermost.

Stepping up to address the ball, he said to himself in that self-hypnotic monotone, "Okay, let's make this a lulu. Head still. Get that body well around. Cock those wrists, and . . ."

"Oh, no!" he exclaimed aghast, as he saw his ball zoom off to the right in a horrendous slice and disappear into the heavily wooded rough. He turned to Hamish, dumbfounded. "What the hell?"

"Head up and right shoulder," said Hamish in much the same manner as a doctor would have diagnosed "uric acid—gout."

"Not your best," said Charles dryly. His own

tee shot was straight and devastatingly long compared to Hubert's. With Pat Hogan at his heels, he strode off toward his drive.

When the two were barely out of earshot, Hubert fumed, "Where were Dan and Bart on that one?"

"Nothing anybody could have done with that wild shot. Besides, the whole system is shut off."

"What do you mean—shut off?" asked Hubert, incredulous.

"Exactly that." Hamish raked his hand over the wood covers in the bag. "These are your regular woods. This bag," and he whacked the side of it, "is your regular bag. The club in your hand is your regular driver. The ball you just hit was a regulation ball that I heated while you were having tea."

Shaking his head in total bewilderment, Hubert immediately tried to push down on the button that loaded the spring of his ED driver, but there was no button to push. This was not his ED driver, yet he vaguely remembered Hamish having appeared to cock it.

Bewilderment gave way to rage. His arm shot out and his fingers clawed at Hamish's elbow. "Just what the hell are you up to?" he snarled.

Hamish turned to face him abruptly, unshoulder-ing the golf bag he carried which, in turn, brushed Hubert's arm aside. Hamish's eyes reflected cold disdain.

"It's no use, Mr. Carnes. I just can't be a party to this devilish scheme of yours."

Hubert instantly adopted the expression of total and complete innocence that had always served him well in Carnesco's dealings with regulatory agencies.

"Just what are you talking about?"

"All along, you've lied to me. This is no secret exercise for the Defense Department. Pat Hogan told me why this match is so important to you. You want to take over this club and Mr. Twitchell's job."

"Pay no attention to Hogan," snapped Hubert. "He's a windbag. He doesn't know what he's talking about."

"He's worked here for thirty-two years, and he says you're trying to do to Mr. Twitchell what Senator Twitchell did to his very own father—to become chairman." Hamish drew himself stiffly erect, the determined soldier prepared to face court-martial rather than carry out the party line. "Well, you're going to have to play out this nine fair and square, strictly on your own without any help from Mr. Costain or Mr. Finch or from me."

The caution chime that had so often saved Hubert J. Carnes in the heat of boardroom passions tinkled warningly in his ear, and instead of coming out with, "You miserable Judas," he asked in strangled voice, "What do you want of me?"

"To play this match as a real golfer—to play the game as I've taught you to play it."

From the corner of his eye, Hubert saw Charles Twitchell walking back toward them, then heard Charles shout through cupped hands, "What's the holdup?"

"Let's find my ball," said Hubert in choked voice, at the same time waving an "everything's okay" hand at Charles. "We can talk this out as we go along."

Hubert's ball proved quite easy to find—almost in the open, but nestled in thick grass and with the extending branches of a large bush draped curtainlike over it.

Hubert gazed at his ball, transfixed. What a terrible lie! What a terrible situation to be in! After not having been off the fairway a single time during the entire first nine, here he was in deep, deep trouble with his very first shot off the tenth.

"Goddamn you, Hamish Taggart," he said through gritted teeth. "Look at the fix I'm in."

"Cursing me won't get you out of there," said Hamish. "But maybe this will." He handed him a nine iron. "Your only hope is to try and punch it out toward the fairway."

After considerable maneuvering, Hubert managed to get to his ball, where he assumed an awkward, crouching position which allowed him just sufficient space for a short backswing. At that moment, Charles Gano Twitchell III chose to appear on the scene to heighten Hubert's discomfiture and chagrin. He could feel his pulse pound. His blood pressure began to mount. Sweat partially blinded him. Summoning all his resolve, he jabbed viciously downward at the ball only to miss it completely.

"Oh, no!" he moaned in anguish and again struck out at the ball in blind fury as if it were a venomous snake he had to decapitate. Miraculously the face of his nine iron somehow connected, and the ball zipped out and sped through a narrow opening in the trees to land on the edge of the rough near the fairway.

Red-faced, trembling, short of breath, Hubert emerged from his ordeal.

"I had a fresh air," he said with a hint of defiance. "I now lie three."

"Yes, I know," replied Charles. His tone was sympathetic. In an effort to apply at least a small Band-Aid to Hubert's tattered pride, he said, "If I had to choose between a fresh air and a shank, I'd take a fresh air every time. At least with a fresh air, you know where your ball is."

Unsmiling, Hubert nodded. Though vaguely appreciative of Charles's intent, how could he be a party to any "grin and bear it" remarks when he was already up to his armpits in despondency? How was he, Hubert J. Carnes, a man his own public-relations division modestly described as "resourceful," "innovative," "a bold visionary," to overcome the perfidy of this damn Scot and the monstrous cunning of Quincetree itself, and still win?

Hamish Taggart had his own idea of how this could be accomplished. "Mr. Carnes, believe me, you can play well enough to win this match, but it must be done fair and square—no more hanky-panky." He indicated the tenth green. "You haven't hope on this hole. Twitchell's already on the green for two, but that still leaves you three up and with six shots in hand. All you have to do is keep your head down and concentrate on that left hip and left hand. See the club head hit through the ball." He handed him his four wood. "Now, let's give it an honest try."

After several deep breaths to partially drain the

rancor from his chest, Hubert did give it an honest try. He did keep his head down. He did see the club head hit through the ball and, as a result, his ball flew straight and true and landed just short of the tenth green.

"Lovely shot," said Hamish and meant it. "You see—it can be done."

"That felt good," admitted Hubert, and somewhere deep inside him the belief kindled that maybe— just maybe—he, Hubert J. Carnes, could, on his own, determine the outcome of this match.

At the short eleventh, Charles had a three. Hubert, strokeless, a four. He was now only two up.

At the 402-yard twelfth, Charles had a four and Hubert a five, but with Hubert's stroke, the hole was halved. He remained two up with six holes left to play.

As they walked off the twelfth green toward the thirteenth tee, Hubert asked Hamish, "Where is my smart bag?"

"Locked in the boot of my car back at the club-house."

——— o ———

Like some squat, buglike creature, the gray van with its revolving radarscope was still parked on Axminister Road.

Inside, Bart's fingers drummed an impatient tattoo on the table top. "Something out there is very wrong," he said.

"That's the second time in four minutes you've made that statement."

"Each passing minute gives the statement greater validity. They've certainly played the tenth and eleventh and possibly finished the twelfth and not a word, not a buzz, nothing. Please play back our last contact."

Dan pushed the "play" button of the tape recorder. Hamish's voice came over the loudspeaker: "They're just finishing tea. As Mr. Carnes is four up at the turn, we'll be using a regulation ball on the tenth, so you won't receive us until the eleventh. Over."

Said Dan, "So, we both interpreted Hamish's words to mean, because Hubert was four up at the turn, it was strategy for him to leave the system, use a regulation golf ball, and let Twitchell win the tenth. That would coincide with the instruction we gave Hamish not to arouse suspicion by abusing the system's potential."

Bart replied, "Then, the only explanation is that they were delayed over tea and somehow, Hubert fluked a half at the tenth. That would still leave him four up." He flashed the card for the second nine at Quincetree upon the computer screen. "Now we come to the short eleventh. The hole is only one hundred and sixty-eight yards long. He could have been on in one and down in two or on in two and down in one for a three and say a half, so he's still four up—still the regulation ball—still no need for the system."

"But why the dead station? Why no acknowledgment?" asked Dan.

Once again, he pressed the system's alert button. "No response."

During the course of the thirteenth hole, Hubert's confidence slowly began to build. On the tee, Hamish had handed him a three wood instead of a driver, and Hubert found this club more to his liking. He used it again for his second shot, and though his ball was well hit, it was still short and to the right of the green.

"That's the way. Play within yourself," encouraged Hamish. "Let the club head do the work." He handed him a nine iron for his third shot. "Head still. Hit through the ball. Good shot!" He pointed to Hubert's divot mark. "See how squarely you hit that ball. You can do it, Mr. Carnes, but you have to slow down and stay down."

Charles's birdie putt on the thirteenth rimmed the cup but spun some eight inches away.

Hubert two-putted, made his five and, with his stroke, halved the hole to remain two up.

"You're not hitting your woods as well as you were on the first nine," commented Charles as they walked toward the fourteenth tee.

Hubert tried to read from Charles's expression if there was some hidden implication behind that remark, but Charles's face reflected only bland good humor.

"No, I'm not," admitted Hubert, "and it worries me."

Hubert would long remember the long, par-five fourteenth hole. There had been a slight fade to Hubert's three wood off the tee, and his ball came to rest in the rough some four feet off the fairway. Hamish handed him an eight wood. He did let the club head do the work, and the ball lifted well out of the thick grass and arched some eighty yards farther onto the fairway.

"Good swing," said Hamish. "You got your duff into that one."

Hubert handed him back the wood. "Go on ahead," he ordered, and with a downward gesture indicated the fly of his pants. "I've got to pee." He walked over to a clump of large oaks and sheltered himself from view. He experienced his usual difficulty in locating his penis and then extracting it from the folds of his shorts. Then, there was the countdown for his bladder to begin to function and the stream to flow. Afterward, there was the jiggling and shaking to verify that his bladder was, in fact, empty. Finally, the necessary juggling to tuck his entire apparatus safely back inside his shorts, then the wiggling to make sure that all was comfortably ensconced, and then the zip up and he was ready. He slowly walked back out into the open, peering down at his pants as he did so to see if, by any chance, he'd spotted himself, but on looking up and fairwayward, he froze in alarm.

Charles and Hamish were standing by Charles's drive some twenty yards ahead and were deep in conversation.

To Hubert, the pose of their bodies suggested clandestine conversation. What were they talking about? What was Hamish showing Charles, for he had the palm of his hand furtively extended outward like some peddler trying to sell a hot watch or ring.

103

Then, as though sensing Hubert's presence, Hamish quickly returned the object to his right pant pocket and swung round to face Hubert. At the same time, he must have alerted Charles, for he, too, turned round. Hamish then started to drift over toward Hubert's ball.

What are those two up to, Hubert wondered . . . too preoccupied with his own dire suspicions to see Charles hit a low, whistling one iron to within five yards of the fourteenth green, but Hamish was not going to permit such a feat to go unnoticed.

"Did you see that great one-iron shot of Mr. Twitchell's?" asked Hamish. "He's only just short of the green for two."

Hubert glanced at him and brusquely asked, "What were you two talking about?"

Hamish registered surprise, not so much at the question, but at the manner in which it was voiced.

"We were talking about the respective merits of the American-size ball compared to the smaller-diameter English ball." He handed him his three wood. "Better take a practice swing, Mr. Carnes. You're looking very tense."

So great was his sense of frustration and impotence, that Hubert was tempted to throw the club to the ground and trample on it, and then he remembered the words of a bronze plaque he had kept for many years on his desk—kept there until he had moved to the splendor of the thirty-sixth floor of Carnesco Tower: IF YOU HAVE THEM BY THE BALLS, THEIR HEARTS AND MINDS WILL FOLLOW. And this damn young Scot had him by the balls and wasn't letting go any more than that damn Twitchell was letting up. Only just short of a par-five hole for two!

Hubert's third was ninety yards short of the green. His fourth was in the nearside bunker protecting the green. His fifth was in that self-same bunker. His sixth came out onto the green in a prodigious shower of sand. He two-putted. His lead was cut to one.

———— O ————

The interior of the gray van parked on Axminister Road was thick with a pervasive gloom.

"One of us has to make a break and find out what's happening," said Bart. "It had better be you. You look respectable enough to be a member of Quincetree."

"Has Hubert left our names at the gate?"

"According to Hubert, we should have no trouble at the gate. The trouble is somewhere out there on the course." Bart handed him a set of car keys. "There is a walkie-talkie in the trunk of Hamish's car. Make contact as soon as you get there. We have to sort this one out and fast."

———— O ————

The fifteenth hole was as disastrous for Hubert as the fourteenth. An astonishing duck hook off the tee sent his ball splashing into Quince Creek. Flustered by the sudden appearance of a duck hook to his already overburdened repertoire of bad shots,

·it took Hubert three more shots to reach the green. This time he two-putted. The match was squared.

"Lucky this isn't a medal round," said Charles with a pompous laugh. "You've dropped six shots in the last two holes."

"I put you down for another four," replied Hubert. "That makes you even figures so far for this nine."

On the short sixteenth, fortune smiled on Hubert for one glorious moment. His tee shot had landed pin high but some four feet to the side of the green, snuggled at the base of a grassy mound. Taking out his putter, Hubert struck the ball in a careless, slap-dash way, but it scampered over the mound, raced across the green to squarely hit the base of the flag stick and plop into the hole for a two. For one exhilarating instant, Hubert believed he was back on the system and that it had been a PS ball that had sped so accurately to the cup; but no—his smart bag was locked in the trunk of Hamish's car and Dan and Bart, God knows where they were and what they were thinking.

From his imposing height, Charles looked disdainfully down on Hubert. His displeasure was evident. In his eyes, Hubert had committed a vulgar fluke. "That puts you one up," he said.

———— O ————

There was tremendous excitement in Dan's voice as it poured out over the van's loudspeakers.

"We're in real trouble here, Bart. I found

Hubert's smart bag in the trunk of Hamish's car. It's in perfect working order. All his ED woods, all his PS balls—but only three infrared balls! What do you make of it? Over."

"It has to be a double cross. Hubert would never let that bag get away from him—even worse, Dan, it could be blackmail. Over."

"That's why I'm locking the smart bag in the trunk of my car. Then I'm going out onto the course and try and find Hubert and Hamish. Over."

"Take the walkie-talkie with you and get back to me as soon as you know anything. Over."

———  O  ———

On the crucial seventeenth, a par five of 504 yards, Hubert struggled valiantly, but without his ED woods, without the system, he could not begin to match Charles Gano Twitchell III's power, distance, and accuracy off the tee and fairway. Even with a stroke, his six to Charles's four was not good enough.

They went to the eighteenth with the match all square.

At first glance, the eighteenth hole at Quincetree appeared a more formidable finishing hole than it really was. The reason—Quince Creek, which later-ally traversed the hole between tee and fairway. The creek itself chortled and gurgled some sixty yards out from an elevated tee. However, on either side of it lay a wasteland of sand, gravel, brush, and several bleached tree trunks with their tangle of roots—scars from spring floods. From the height of the tee, one looked across this inhospitable terrain to a wide ribbon of green fairway, a carry of 158 yards, a sight to traumatize the faint of heart.

Once across this forbidding natural hazard, the fairway ascended and narrowed to a table-top green whose entrance was frontally protected by bunkers to the left and right. The green itself was rectangular in shape with the shorter side of the rectangle abutting the fairway. The green was designed to accommodate only very straight, accurate iron shots from the fairway. The steep banks on either side of the table top assured any ball that did not hold the green a tumbling descent to ignominy and thick grass at the bottom of the bank.

The late Senator Twitchell had named the hole "The Bitter Quince."

"It's always a great match that is decided on the last hole," said Charles. He swung a three wood loosely back and forth. "But I warn you, Hubert—I intend to win this hole." Looking toward the eighteenth green, he smiled wickedly. "A four might just do it; a three certainly would."

Teeing his ball low, Charles, with that easy, effortless swing of his, laced the ball straight out and over Quince Creek and onto the fairway and up to within five-iron range of the green.

"Your best of the day," said Pat Hogan.

"Fine shot," said Hamish.

The lump of despair in Hubert's throat prevented him from speaking. The best he could manage was a wan nod of agreement. Without question, Charles had hit an awesome shot. He took the three wood Hamish handed him. "The Bitter Quince—The Bitter End," thought Hubert. Now, after months of planning, practicing, and how many millions of wasted dollars, all had to be decided on one hole, the last hole, and with the odds in favor of Charles Gano Twitchell III.

He looked out over Quince Creek and shuddered. How many times in the past had his drive failed to carry that damn creek? If ever he needed the help of an ED wood, it was now, but thanks to that traitor, that Judas, that two-faced son of a bitch Hamish Taggart, he stood alone without any other resource than his bare hands and his animal instinct for survival; but on one thing he was resolved—no matter how this game ended, he was firing Hamish's ass back to Scotland and hopefully in chains.

He tried a practice swing. It felt awkward and uncomfortable. He tried another only to realize his hands were sweaty. He took the towel from his belt, wiped off his hands, and wiped off the grip of the club. He walked over and addressed his ball as well as himself. "Thrust out those arms. Elbows close together. Feel those last three fingers of your left hand. Head still. Slow turn. Cock those wrists."

Hubert lunged at the ball as if to catch it by surprise. "Oh, no!" he exclaimed in horror as his ball sped straight toward the creek, clearing it by a scant two feet to hit the top of a boulder and to ricochet upward in a high arc, and then to leap forward onto the edge of the fairway.

"Did you see that!" exclaimed Hubert, amazed. He turned to them. "Did you see that incredible shot?"

"This is my seventeen hundred and thirty-sixth

round here," said Charles, "and I have yet to see a shot like that."

"Maybe this is my day after all," thought Hubert, relieved at his miraculous escape from the hazards of "Bitter Quince," yet, as he walked across the wooden bridge that spanned the entire width of the creek bed, his sweat-soaked shirt plastered to his back, a tight band of anxiety began to press across his forehead. His worries settled even heavier on his shoulders, and they slumped under the pressure. His step slowed. How was he ever going to scramble a four? His drive was only just on the fairway. He was such a long way from the green.

On reaching his ball, he commanded Hamish, "Give me my two wood."

Hamish raised a protesting hand. "Use your head, Mr. Carnes. No matter what club you use, you're never going to reach that green in two. You have to play for position. Here, take this four wood and concentrate on seeing the club face hit through the ball."

Appreciating that Hamish spoke the truth, Hubert took the proffered club and addressed the ball. He could hear the murmuring of Quince Creek behind him. Everywhere else, stillness. He sensed that Charles was intently watching him. He began his incantation. "Easy does it. Feel that left hand. Get that big ass of yours around. Head still."

"Fine shot!" said Hamish approvingly. "You kept your head down on that one."

"Well struck," added Charles, and then walked up the fairway to his ball. After studying his lie, he looked twice and carefully from ball to green and from green to ball. He then threw a pinch ot grass into the air to test the wind. There was a slight breeze against him. He said more to Pat Hogan than to Hubert or Hamish. "I wish the stick wasn't so far forward. It doesn't give me much room to work with." He pulled out a five iron and regarded it with esteem. Turning to Hamish, he said, "Did I tell you that your great-uncle Finnie forged this club for me?" He ran his thumb across the blade of the club. "After a while, you tend to believe in certain clubs and what they can do for you."

Suddenly, he became very serious, very intent. To him, this had to be the most important shot of the day. He had to put the ball close enough to the stick to give himself a reasonable chance of a birdie. He struck the ball perfectly, and as it flew greenward, Hubert, following its flight with trepidation, saw it as his doom shot; yet on hitting the top edge of the green, instead of bouncing onward toward the flag, the ball pitched backward and trickled down into the bunker.

"Damn!" exclaimed Charles, and there was real pain in his voice.

"You didn't deserve that," said Pat Hogan.

"What an unlucky kick," said Hamish.

Hubert tried hard to mask his jubilation. "Tough break," he said, but the corners of his mouth twisted upward as he said it.

When they reached Hubert's ball, Hamish handed him a nine iron. "Don't be afraid to hit a full shot. You want to get the ball high in the air and drop it on the green."

Nodding in understanding, Hubert did an instant

recap of the status of the game, which only served to tense his muscles and shorten his breath with excitement. Charles was in the bunker for two. If only he, Hubert, were to put his third shot close to the pin for a net two, then there was a chance, a good chance, of victory, sweet, sweet victory.

As he waggled the nine iron back and forth in preparation for the critical blow, Hubert kept repeating softly to himself, "Hip and left hand, hip and left hand," but somewhere en route to his brain, that message short-circuited; for at the very top of his backswing, he pushed his right shoulder hard into the shot, up came his head, and the face of the nine iron dug deep into the ground. It was only the resultant shuddering eruption of the earth's surface that caused his ball to move three inches forward.

Appalled at the havoc his own hand had wrought, Hubert stepped back from the ball and looked down at the deep, ugly gouge he had made in the fairway. The face of his nine iron was caked with earth. He handed the club to Hamish, who shoveled the blade clean with his thumb and then wiped it off with a towel. Hubert stood transfixed in shock. He had just played three, and he was only three inches closer to the green. He found it difficult to reconcile what the Lord had given him with his tee shot at the eighteenth and what the Lord had just taken away with that simple short iron to the green.

Handing him back the nine iron, Hamish said in the patient manner of a parent talking to a retarded child, "I want you to take a few practice swings with your left hand only—just as you used to do at our

first lessons. See if you can't get back the feel of hip and left hand."

When Hubert was finally ready to again address the ball, Hamish's last word of advice was, "Be sure and hit through the ball."

Knowing that of all the golf shots he had ever played in all his years of playing golf this one shot was by far the most important, Hubert—lips pressed hard together in determination—struck the ball flawlessly to have it fly high in the air and drop dead seven feet from the pin.

"Beautiful shot," said Hamish. "I'm proud of you."

"I'm kind of proud of that myself," replied Hubert, dazedly.

"Lovely shot," commented Charles, his urbanity intact, still wearing that insufferable air of supreme confidence. However, Charles had a difficult lie. His ball was nestled tight against the lip of the bunker. Not a shot to be pampered, Charles played it masterfully, but to assure that his ball came out cleanly, he had to strike it hard. It sailed out of the bunker to land at the very back of the green, a good forty feet from the flag.

It was a happier Hubert Carnes who walked onto the eighteenth green, his body buoyant and weightless, a warm, euphoric glow pulsing through his entire being. He lay net three to Charles's gross three, but Charles's ball was at least forty feet away, a good two putts away, maybe three. He had done it! He had not only survived, he was but a scant seven feet from one-putt victory and what a bounteous victory—

chairman and captain of the last citadel of the gentleman golfer—the Carnesco Open, the richest purse
in golf—the Carnesco Garden Condominiums, three
bedrooms, four baths, each with its own spacious verandah facing lovely Quince Creek and the historic
Quincetree Golf Club.  Everything he had always
wanted in a putt and more.

Charles placed a marker behind his ball, then
lifted it and pocketed it.  Hubert did the same.  Then,
putter in hand, Charles slowly walked alongside the
path his putt would follow, carefully scrutinizing the
green.  He retraced his steps and, hunkering down
directly behind his marker, again studied the contour
of the green.  Rising to his feet, he said in a loud,
clear voice, "Now would seem as good a time as any
to try that new ball you gave me, Hamish."

He withdrew a ball from his pocket.

A cold chill of apprehension began to seep
through Hubert's veins, numbing his muscles, short-
ening his breath, accelerating his heartbeat.

Holding up the ball close to his eyes and revolv-
ing it slowly like a jeweler examining a gemstone,
Charles asked in an equally loud voice, "What does
*PS* stand for?"

"Putting Surface," replied Hamish, without hesi-
tation.

Try as he might, Hubert could not stifle the moan
of anguish that Hamish's words wrenched from him.

Charles placed his ball in the exact position of
the marker.  He turned to face Hubert.

"I must be about the same distance from the pin
that you were on the fifth when you sank that magnificent putt."

"Christ, he knows!" Hubert's stomach began to churn, a burning mixture of nausea, rage, and panic. "That two-faced bastard Hamish has sold me out—ruined me!"

Charles took two perfunctory practice putts before stepping up to his ball. After a moment's study of the line of his putt, he stroked the ball firmly, crisply.

In fascinated horror, Hubert watched his child of high technology—the child his money had sup ported during the formative months of infancy—speed unerringly toward the hole and plop in with a dreadful finality.

With a jaunty nonchalance, as though sinking a forty footer was really not that difficult, Charles Gano Twitchell III walked up to the hole and retrieved his ball.

Consternation propelled Hubert across the green.

"Let me see that ball," he demanded in a hoarse voice.

"Why, of course," replied Charles easily, and handed it to him. "It's the same Titleist 3 I've been using all morning."

Hubert gaped incredulously at the ball as he turned it over and over in his hand. It was not a PS ball. It was, indeed, a regulation Titleist and bore the perceptible marks and stains of hard play.

The realization that he had been tricked by his own latent guilt and by that lucky putt, or had it been a predestined putt of retribution, sickened Hubert. He found it hard to control the trembling of his lips, the twitching of his hand as he handed the ball back to Charles. "I'm sorry. This match has me really uptight."

Towering over him like some stern-faced bailiff, Charles took Hubert firmly by the elbow and marched him off to the courtroom—the edge of the green—out of earshot of Hamish and Pat Hogan. His normally soft blue eyes had frosted over to a steely gray. His tone was contemptuous.

"From what little Hamish has told me, your conduct this morning has been utterly disgraceful, that you have deliberately broken every rule of golf and every rule of sportsmanship."

Aware he was now fighting for his life, Hubert countered, "I can't believe you'd listen to the lies of some damn foreigner. That man is trying to blackmail me."

"I have every confidence in the integrity of any great-nephew of Finnie Taggart. Besides, he states he has evidence of illegal clubs, illegal balls, and even an illegal golf bag, although I can't conceive of such a thing, safely under lock and key."

Hubert remembered asking Hamish, "Where's my smart bag?" and his reply, "Locked in the boot of my car back at the clubhouse." In his best chairman and chief executive officer of Carnesco, a conglomerate of ten companies, manner, he blustered, "Charles, I'm not prepared to demean myself by discussing such absurd charges at this time. I concede the hole. You've won the match. You're still captain and still chairman." He turned to leave.

Charles Gano Twitchell III placed a heavy restraining hand on Hubert's arm. "Oh, no you don't," he said. "If you leave this green without putting out, I shall see that you are expelled forthwith from this club for conduct unbecoming to a gentleman and to a member. Furthermore, I shall see to it that such expulsion is given the widest publicity."

Hubert remembered Max's words: "All I know is that in those posh, goy clubs, you can sleep with another member s wife and nobody cares, but if you cheat at golf or cards, they'll sling your ass out onto the street. They'll pillory you."

"What is it you want?" asked Hubert, his soul's deep despair reflected in his voice.

"From what Hamish has told me, I'm not unmindful that for these last nine holes, you've tried to play the game as it should be played, nor am I unmindful of the contribution you've made to Quincetree over the years. Therefore, I'm prepared to go along with Hamish's request."

Bewilderment clouded Hubert's face. "Hamish's request?"

"Yes, to truly test you as a golfer and as a man." Charles pushed his right forefinger deep into Hubert's chest to spear his total attention. "If you sink that putt and the match is halved, then nothing will be said. The evidence will be returned to you. You will continue as vice-captain of this club until my son takes over, and starting tomorrow, Hamish Taggart will become Quincetree's assistant greenkeeper, reporting to Pat Hogan."

Hubert looked up at Charles and asked in quavering voice, "And if I don't make the putt?"

"Then, Hamish turns the evidence over to me,

**117**

and he leaves for Scotland tomorrow. It will then be up to the trustees to decide how we will deal with you."

Mesmerized by Charles's unblinking, unforgiving stare, Hubert said softly to himself, "Jesus, between the rock and the hard place." With a gesture of capitulation, he turned and walked back across the green to where Hamish was standing.

"I'll take my putter," he said, conscious of how stiffly upright Hamish stood and how unwavering and rebellious was his look.

"It's a straight putt, Mr. Carnes. Firm and to the back of the cup. You're against the nap."

Hubert walked over to where his marker impaled the green; lifting it, he placed his ball precisely where the marker had been. He looked down at his ball. It lay about seven feet from the hole. Everything he had ever wanted in a putt and less. A great weariness settled over him. He felt drained. Never had he felt quite so alone. As his back was to Hamish, Charles and Pat, he did not see Dan Finch hurry up onto the edge of the green, only to be stopped in his tracks by Charles, interposing his bulk between Dan and the green and putting a finger to his lips to warn Dan not to disturb Hubert as he putted.

Flexing and unflexing his fingers' grip on the putter, a jumbled disarray of thoughts flashed across Hubert's mind with a thousand times the speed of a computer printout.

"Did you ever in your wildest think it would come to this? Everything—and, brother, I mean everything—riding on a seven-foot putt. And after all you

**118**

spent with those two Leonardo da Vincis, you wind up using an ordinary golf ball that anybody can buy for less than two dollars. But if you make this putt, you could crawl out smelling like a rose—and there's got to be a way to break old Twitch's lock on this club. And what about the hold he has on you, smart ass? If only you can get your hands on that bag. Then, it would be just Hamish's word against yours. And what a goddamn do-gooder he turned out to be!" He shook his head. "Cut it, Hubie! Concentrate! This is the one putt you can't blow. Dead straight and against the nap. Let's try taking the putter back smoothly. Not like that, stupid! Try again. There. That's better. One more time. Okay—you're as ready to go as you'll ever be. The formula: head still—club face square—firm stroke—see the blade strike the ball—follow through. The golden rule—wait to hear the ball drop."

Crouched well over the ball, his head anchored in place, Hubert J. Carnes took the putter blade back smoothly. The club face squarely met the ball. The ball rolled forward. Head bowed, as though in silent prayer, he waited, listening for the ball to drop.

———— o ————

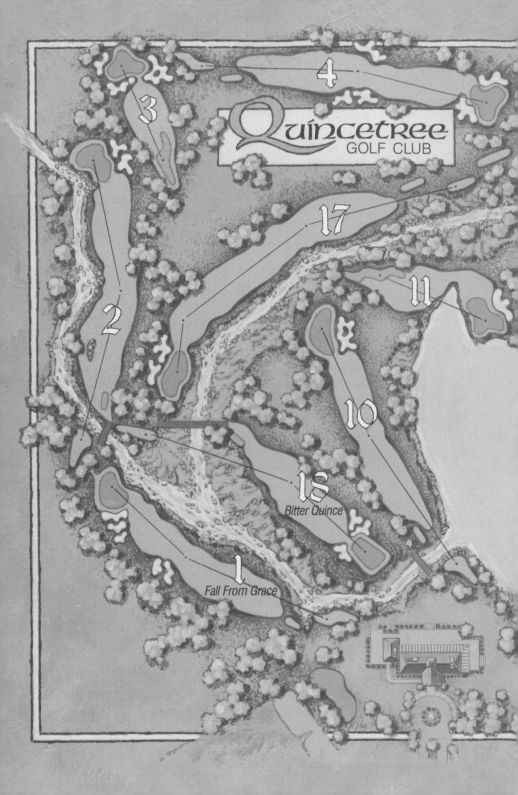